Anonymous

The Adventures of Fearless Fred

The Outlaw

Anonymous

The Adventures of Fearless Fred
The Outlaw

ISBN/EAN: 9783337337179

Printed in Europe, USA, Canada, Australia, Japan

Cover: Foto ©Andreas Hilbeck / pixelio.de

More available books at **www.hansebooks.com**

NEW YORK:
DICK & FITZGERALD, PUBLISHERS

FEARLESS FRED;

THE HIGHWAYMAN

OF

HOUNSLOW HEATH.

CHAPTER I.

FIRST APPEARANCE OF FEARLESS FRED.

SOME years ago, on a raw November day, there was considerable stir in the neigborhood of St. Giles on account of a fine looking male child that had been found singularly stowed away in one corner of the top-row of a celebrated beer show.

Old Boniface, whose name was Ralph Jewel—and a jewel of an old boy he was—appeared so anxious to deny the paternity of the foundling that many a black-eyed lass who frequented that part of London dared to suspect that he knew more about the matter than he was willing to confess, and that, notwithstanding the fact that there was no more resemblance between the supposed father and the child than there is between a noble war-horse and an asthmatic pair of bellows.

The sly winks and wise looks that passed from one to the other exasperated old Jewel beyond all bounds. He stamped about the floor with his wooden leg, and fire shot from his one red eye, as if he was ready to do battle with a host in defence of his innocence.

"But what will you do with the lad?" inquired Botany Bay Nell—a strapping lass who had just returned from a seven years' transportation—as she placed her arms a-kimbo and straddled in front of the indignant landlord.

"Throw him into the Thames!" cried mine host thrusting out his wooden leg and bringing the end of it down on the floor with such violence as to make all the glasses and empty decanters ring again.

"That you shall not," cried Nell, picking up the urchin and stowing him into a big basket as if he had been a wadding of dirty clothes. "I will take charge of the brat as if I was his mother, and who knows but when I have given him an education and brought him up in the way he should go, he may take care of me in my old age, and bring me in the blunt, when I am too old to——"

"To take dummies for yourself," interrupted Ralph Jewel—"ha! ha! ha when you get too old for that, Nell, it will be because scragging has gone clear out of date. You were never born to make old bones; and the devil help the brat after the bringing up that you will give him. But take him along, Nell; he might have fell into worse hands"—the last words being added on account of a tiger-like expression of the eyes which the lusty girl cast upon her interlocutor, and also the fact that Nell was no indifferent customer at the Black Horse Shoe.

From that moment, nothing was heard of the foundling in that corner of the city of London, except that he was named Frederick and was regularly sent to the parish school by Nell Pritthand, commonly known as Botany Bay Nell—a euphonious title by which she was known in her absence, though few cared to give her that appellation when within earshot of the strapping graduate of New Holland.

CHAPTER II.

FEARLESS FRED AND JANE—THE CEDAR BOX.

It was about nineteen years from the period in which our scene opens, that a *fracas* occurred in the streets of London, at the hour of midnight, which caused no little alarm to the denizens in the immediate neighborhood of the transaction.

Loud cries were heard, expressive of great wrath on the part of some of the parties, while from the midst of the uproar went up one solitary, wild scream in which the voice of a female was detected.

On hastening to the spot, the watchman found a well-dressed young woman of some eighteen or twenty years of age in the hands of half a dozen ruffians, while a young fellow, neatly dressed as a seaman was belaboring them with a cudgel, and endeavoring to rescue the girl from their clutches. By the aid of the watchman, this was quickly done, and

then the girl sprang into the arms of the young fellow whom she very affectionately called her dear Fred.

"Jane," said he, "you are not hurt, I hope?" Before she could reply, a tall raw-boned fellow who had just released the girl from his grasp on a hint from the watchman's club, came up and demanded the youth as a common highwayman, and declared that he had stolen the girl from the house of a certain Countess, and he was come to recapture her; to which the girl replied—"no—no—the Countess is my enemy, and has ill-treated me. I will go with Fred."

Before anything more could be said, the young man and the girl walked off together.

"I am Peter Bayley," said the tall man, "and have been sent with these officers to apprehend the girl and return her to the Countess from whom she has escaped," and he pointed to three men who came clustering around him. But it was too late. Fred and Jane had turned the first corner, and though the watchman went a little way with Bayley and his men to look for them, they were not to be found.

"You are Peter Bayley, the famous thief-taker," said one of the watchmen. "Why did you not say it at the time, and things might have turned up differently?"

"You know who I am now," said Peter Bayley, "and this night's work will cost you dear. There have slipped out of my hands two of the most abandoned wretches in all England. Look out for yourselves, I shall remember you."

The watchmen skulked off with eyes cast down, and yet with low mutterings which denoted that although the notorious thief-taker might be feared, yet he was also hated quite as much as he was dreaded.

Leaving Peter Bayley to curse his

stars and the intrusive charleys, we will follow upon the footsteps of the young couple, and see what became of them. They ran, rather than walked, along the silent streets of the city, something less than two miles, when they reached an old house, constructed in the ancient style standing in the midst of a wide green, and partly surrounded by lime trees and elms.

Having tapped at the door, it was opened to them by a man in a blue coat and corduroy pants, who hurried them in and shut the door quickly.

" Well, Blake,' said the youth, " what is the news?"

"Nothing except that Peter Bayley and his men have been watching this house all the afternoon, and I think it pretty certain that he knows the cedar box is concealed within its walls."

" Then no time is to be lost," said Fred. "Here are two young girls who are thrown, by circumstances upon my protection. This one," pointing to a tall young woman who was in the house, " has need to keep out of sight for a few days, while my Jane here has every reason to dread the unprincipled Bayley. This cedar box certainly contains something of vast importance to Jane, and must be kept out of the clutches of Peter Bayley, whose very eagerness to seize it, affords presumptive evidence that some wrong is intended towards Jane. The treatment that she has received from the Countess, from whom she has fled, is another proof that a plot of some kind is hatching against her peace. At least, we cannot venture out again together."

"No; you would be certain to encounter him or some of his myrmidons. You must hide yourself until his visit of inspection is over. I have been with him in this house before, and I noticed that there was a narrow staircase that leads to a flat part of the roof at the top

of it. There, I think you will be in perfect security, for Bayley has no motive to take him up there, and his time is too much occupied for him to go merely for the view of old Islington that he would get from that place."

" Hush !" said Fred. " What is that ?"

" What do you hear ?"

" The tread of horses' feet in the street, unless I am much mistaken."

" Then it is Peter himself."

Blake flew to the street door, and shot one of the bolts into its socket.

" He can't get in now," he said, " until I open the door to him. Get your friends to go at once to the hiding place I have mentioned."

" I will. Come this way."

Fred led Blake into the back parlor, and quieted the alarm that his sudden appearance gave to Jane and Eliza, by saying—

" This is a friend. He warns us of the approach of Peter Bayley ; we must hide ourselves at once."

" Oh," said Blake, " what will he think of this breakfast set out here ?"

" Say it is yours," said Fred., as he caught up two of the tea-cups and threw them into the fire. "There is but one cup now, and he may think that you liked to make yourself comfortable."

" I will try so to impose upon him, but that must not be any hindrance to your hiding. Follow me at once."

Bang ! came a knock at the door, and then it was followed by a rattling peal at the bell, which Bayley had found out the position of, although it was so secretly placed as to completely elude all ordinary observation ; but the prying eyes of Peter were not easily to be deceived.

" Quick—quick !" said Blake.

Fred assisted Jane, and Eliza followed as well as she could, and they all got to the upper story of the house with tolerable expedition. Eliza knew very well the door that opened to a spiral staircase leading to the flat leads at the top of the house, and in the course of half a minute more they had all three passed through the little door, and Blake was hurrying down stairs again, for Bayley had knocked with such fury as showed him that it seemed as if he were determined to have the door down if no one came quickly in answer to his summons.

Blake was almost breathless with the haste that he made when he flung the door open. Peter Bayley, with four men at his heels, made a rush into the passage.

"What's the meaning of this?" he cried. "Why am I kept waiting at the door? Is there any trickery going on here?"

"Trickery, sir?"

"Yes. That was the word. I said trickery, and I mean it."

"He would need to be a bold man, Mr. Bayley, that would try anything like trickery towards you, sir. I am not yet tired of my life. The fact is, there is an old mulberry-tree in the garden, and I was looking at it, and could not get to the door very soon."

"So it seems."

"Did you knock more than once, sir?"

"You know I did."

"It isn't for me to contradict you, Mr. Bayley; but the fact is, that I don't know anything of the sort. I heard a knock that was enough to batter the door down, and a violent ring; but I heard nothing before that."

"Bah!"

"Very good, sir."

The four officers who were with Bayley, could not help smiling at the imperturbable coolness of Blake; and Bayley, after regarding him now for a few minutes in silence, said—

"How long have you been here?"

"About an hour, sir."

"Liar! you were seen at the end of the street not a quarter of an hour ago."

"Oh, yes."

"And yet you say you have been here an hour?"

"I don't deny that I went out to get a drop of milk to take with my breakfast, as I had got it all nicely and snugly ready before it struck nine, for I could not take it without"

"Oh, indeed. And, pray, where did you prepare this nice and snug breakfast, Mr. Blake?"

"In the back parlor, sir."

"Indeed! We shall soon see whether or not there is any truth in that. You ought to have been here an hour and more ago, for I sent you; but by the devil I doubt you, Mr. Blake."

"Certainly, sir, by all means."

"Curse this house," muttered Bayley. "and all that were ever in it. It is an eye-sore to me, and every time I come to it I am inclined to set light to it, but that I still suspect there are secrets hidden within its old walls that I want to get at. Oh, for that cedar box! Hark you, my men!"

"Yes, Mr. Bayley," said the officers

"There is a small cedar box, containing papers that I want very particularly; I have some reason to believe that it is still hidden in this house somewhere, notwithstanding the search I have already made in it, and I hear offer a hundred pound note for it if any of you can find it. Don't let a hole or corner escape you, and I will wait for you in this room."

CHAPTER III
ANOTHER DISAPPOINTMENT.

BLAKE knew as well as possible, ay, as well as if Peter Bayley had whispered

the fact into his ear, that he was mistrusted, and that, although Bayley had
a notion that he was a man of ability,
that he would not scruple for a moment
to put him to death, as there was every
reason to believe he had done to others.

While these things were going on below, Fred and the two girls had ascend-
ed to the roof where they escaped the
prying eyes of Peter Bayley and his
officers who, after searching every spot
in the old mansion, took their departure with much grumbling and awful
swearing on the part of Peter Bayley.
As soon as they were gone, Fred descended from the roof with the girls,
and while the latter remained under the
protection of Blake, the former repaired
to the cellar.

After groping his way some minutes
in this damp and mouldy region, he came
to a spot in one corner upon which lay
a small flat stone, having removed which,
he began to dig up the earth with a rusty
case knife which he found near the spot.
After a time, the knife struck against
something hard, and then laying down
the knife, he used his fingers to remove
the loose earth.

In another minute, he drew from the
mouldy soil a small box, at which he
evinced great joy. He exclaimed with
delight, as he felt the box—"it's here,
and I live and breathe again. All's
right. I must have buried it deeper
than I thought, or it has worked down
through the damp ground of its own ac-
cord. Never mind, so long as I have it."

With the precious box——for Fred
could not but believe that it was precious
in some way—clutched to his breast, he
began to ascend the stairs. He heard
the rats screaming in hideous chorus,
and far off in the obscurity of the cellar he now saw some hundreds of their
eyes glaring at him. They seemed to
have collected in force, as though they

had really, as those creatures will do at
times, met to attack him, and try to over-
power him by numbers.

"Take that," said Fred as he threw
the still red-hot stick among them, and
then the scampering that ensued, and
the squeaking, convinced him that it
had gone among a mob of them."

In another moment, Fred was in the
passage.

"I have it—I have it!" he cried.

"Thank God for that," said Jane.

"And so say I," cried Blake. "Let
us leave this place."

Fred placed Jane's arm within his
own, and smiling upon her, he said—

"Dear Jane, you shall not now for another moment be exposed to the terrors
of this house. I know that to you they
must be very great and serious; but
come away, dear one, and never mind
the past. I have a hope that in this
mysterious little box is contained information of the greatest importance. Open
the door, Blake."

"With pleasure," said Blake.

The street door was opened, and out
they all four sallied into the street.—
Fred thought for a moment, and then
turning to the right, he said,

"Let us go this way at once. It
don't matter whether we go east, west,
north or south, so that we get away from
this place, and leave as great a distance
between us and Peter Bayley as possible.'

"That is it," said Blake. "We have
only that man to dread in all the world.
Oh, would that he were no more. They
do say that he has sold himself to the
devil, and has a charmed life."

"Stuff!" said Fred. If Peter had
sold himself to old Nick he would have
made a better bargain than he has; and,
besides, you don't suppose that the devil
would be so stupid as to buy any one
that, in the regular course of nature, he
would be sure to have for nothing?"

"Fred," said Jane, as she pressed his arm, "I don't like to hear you talk in that strain."

"Then I won't."

"You will oblige me very much, indeed, by so doing, Fred. It may be prejudice in me, but I dislike levity upon anything that has a tendency to produce thoughts of an hereafter."

"That's a capital sermon," said Fred, laughing, "and I stand convicted accordingly. On—on. Let us get out of breath the first mile, and then we can go as easy as you all like."

To tell the truth, they none of them wanted much urging to get out of the neighborhood of that dismal old house.

"I wish I had set fire to the old house, Jane."

"Oh, no—no!"

"Why not?"

"There are neighbours, you know, Fred and they might have suffered."

There is no knowing what sort of disclosure Fearless Fred's modesty might have induced him to make, but he was cut short in his reply by seeing a lady on horseback approaching, followed by a groom in very rich livery, indeed. The lady was passing on, but at the sight of Jane, she uttered an exclamation, which induced her to look round, and then she seemed to be quite as much struck by the appearance of Jane as Jane had been at her.

"Good Heavens!" cried the lady. "It is——"

She was evidently upon the point of pronouncing some name, but prudence restrained it upon her lips. She rode up to Fred and Jane, and in a voice, the agitation of which was so great that she could hardly speak articulately, she said, or rather tried to say—

"Who are you, young man, and what do you do in the society of this girl, whose protector I am?"

"Oh, no, no!" said Jane. "Fred, this is the countess who so cruelly persecuted me, and from whom you rescued me."

"Girl, girl!" cried the countess, for it was, indeed that rather unscrupulous personage. "Girl, what do you mean? Nothing but ignorance can induce you to speak in such a strain. Come with me this moment. I tell you now, once and for all, that I have a right to command you."

"Jane," said Fred, with all the coolness in the world, "are you sure of the identity of this woman?"

"Oh, yes, yes!" said Jane. "I know her too well."

"Who is it that dares to address such language to me?" cried the countess. "Woman, indeed!"

"Madam," said Fred, "I really beg your pardon if you are not a woman. To be sure, your conduct towards this young girl was anything but womanly; but I am very glad to have met you."

"Indeed, rascal! and what for?"

"Because I shall hold you fast till I can give you into the custody of the police, on a charge of stealing this girl from her home, and tempting her to commit a serious offence against the law."

Fred laid hold of the horse by the bit as he spoke, and for a moment or two her ladyship was evidently too much amazed and enraged to reply to him. Then she struck him with her riding whip, upon which Fred snatched it from her hands and broke it in two, casting the fragments to the ground.

"I believe you are a woman," he said, "although you deny it; but if I had believed you were not, I would have rammed that riding whip down your throat."

"Insolent wretch! William—William, I say! Where's my groom? Where is William?"

"Oh," said Blake, "he's all right, my lady."

Upon this, Fred looked in the direction whence Blake's voice came from, and he saw that he was pointing a pistol at the head of the groom, whose hat had fallen off, and whose hair was standing on end with terror, lest he should be shot.

"William!" cried the countess, "are you going to see me stopped and maltreated and robbed on the highway, and do nothing?"

"Beg pardon, my lady," said William, "but this gentleman with the long pistol says as he will blow my head off if I come to you or make any alarm; and as it is the only head I've got, my lady, I would rather be a little careful of it, you see, my lady."

"Cowardly rascal!"

"Ah, that's all very well, my lady, but a pistol is a pistol. Them as lives to run away—fights and lives another day. That ain't quite the right words, but they lets you know, my lady, what I means."

"Now, madam," said Fred, as he let go the countess' bridle. Now, madam, if you were to live to the age of the patriarchs, and if you were to paint an inch thick, I should know you again; so you may go."

"Jane!" cried the countess, "I command you to come with me."

"I have no reason to obey you, countess," said Jane. "I do not know you but as the female who persecuted me, and who played the part of my jailor. I despise and defy you!"

"Bravo!" said Blake. "Fred!"

"What is it?"

"Come closer to me. I want to say something to you, if you please."

Fred stepped up close to Blake, who whispered in his ear—.

"The horses, Fred—would they not

be handy? They are good ones; besides, as a general thing, it isn't wise to leave your foes mounted and yourself on foot."

"True—true. I did not think of that."

"Well, it is worth thinking of. We can carry off both the girls, you know. You can take charge of Miss Jane, and I of the other."

"It shall be done. You get possession of the groom's horse, and I will take the countess's."

"Good."

Blake had no difficulty with the groom, for he was so thoroughly frightened, that if he had been ordered to stand on his head, he would at all events have made the attempt; nor did Fred meet with much difficulty from the countess, for suddenly laying hold of her, he had her off the horse in a minute, notwithstanding her cries for help.

"Hold the horse's head, Jane," cried Fred, for the countess would not let go of him, and began to use her nails, with rather more freedom than was at all pleasant, upon his face.

"Confound you!" said Fred. "I don't want to hurt you, but you had better be quiet. You won't? Go there, then, and I advise you not to stir, or plump you will go into a ditch."

By an effort of strength that was almost too much for him, Fred lifted the countess to the height of a very broad-topped thorn-hedge that was by the side of the road, and fairly laid her on her back on the top of it. Her weight made her sink down a little, so that she was incapable of helping herself in the least, and with only the liberty of squalling to any extent.

"Stop her bawling," cried Blake.

"I can't do that," said Fred. "Let us be off out of ear-shot of it, and then we shall be rid of it."

Jane was mounted upon the countess's horse by Fred, who sprang up behind her, and Blake took care of the young girl, so that they set off at a capital pace into the country, leaving her ladyship and the groom lamenting.

CHAPTER IV.

FRED IS OUTGENERALED FOR ONCE IN A WAY.

SUCH a chance as this which had befallen Fred and his friends was hardly to have been looked for, and, indeed, the whole affair had been so bewilderingly rapid, that Jane could hardly take upon herself to say what had happened, ere she was galloped off at a rate that was enough to take her breath away.

"Oh, Fred—Fred," she said, "would it not have been better to let that woman go as we met with her?"

"Certainly not, my dear Jane. You may depend that she and her groom would only have ridden so far till they had met with some assistance, and then we should have had them after us."

They had taken a road which led them towards Stamford Hill, and as he went on, Fred began to ask himself what was to become of Jane.

A more painful question than that he could not conceive, for he felt that it would be an iniquitous thing of him to keep her with him; and yet how to dispose of her troubled him much.

"Jane," he said.

"Yes, Fred."

"I am thinking that you ought to be placed in some home where you would be free from all the terrors that beset my mode of life."

Jane began to cry.

"Nay, now," said Fred, "I——"

"Fred—Fred!" cried Blake, at this moment, "we are pursued. Look over the hedge to your left, and tell me what you see in the fields yonder."

Fred did look, and he saw a party of eight men on horseback, coming along at a good pace. The dress and the general appearance of these men were quite sufficient to fix them as officers of the police.

"Nabbed, I'm afraid," said Fred.

"Oh, no—no!" cried Jane.

"A stern chase, you know, Fred," said Blake, "is a long chase."

"Speak, Fred," said Jane; "what would you have me do?"

"In plain language, then," said Fred, "if I am taken, it will be half of it owing to my anxiety concerning you, Jane, preventing me from taking those measures to save myself, which otherwise might be afforded. Do you understand me? I would have you leave me."

"Fred, where am I to go?"

"Trust to Blake. Take this money Now, don't cry. Take this little cedar box, too, and guard it with your life. It may be that this is the second time that I have had it in my possession, and yet have been unable to look at it. It is rather strange and provoking that it should be so, for all that."

"No—no!"

"Yes, Jane. Do not let me hear you say no. There is a cluster of cottages in front of us. Stop, there, and all three of you go into one of them and ask for a little rest. I will ride on."

"But how shall we meet again?"

"If I escape, I will be to-night, at the hour of twelve, at Tottenham Cross. Blake will know the place well enough; but if I am not there at the time, you may depend that something has happened."

"Oh, Fred, you had better kill me."

"Had I though? I am of a very different opinion, and when I tell you that

I think my chances of escape depend upon your obeying my instructions in this matter, I don't think you ought to hesitate."

After this sort of appeal to her, what could Jane say? It was quite impossible that she could resit it. If she did, she must either say that she set up her own judgment in opposition to Fred's, and that she did not believe that he run more risk with her than without her, or she must say that she was indifferent to that fact.

It was not likely that the gentle and affectionate girl would embrace either of these propositions, so she said, at once—

" Fred, be it as you will."

" That is right, Jane

They were within a hundred yards or so of a very pretty little cottage, the garden of which was laid out with exceeding taste and neatness. It was there that Fred wished Jane to go. •

" But do you think they will be kind enough to allow us to wait there ?" said Jane, mournfully.

" I know, they are a good sort of people."

" You know it, Fred. ? How is that?"

" Why, look at that cat there on the lawn, sitting upon a little square piece of carpet that she seems quite to think her own. They would not be indulgent to that creature if they had not hearts, those people. You may lay it down as a rule, Jane, that folks who love animals are of the kind and considerate order, and they are pretty sure not to disappoint you."

" I believe it, Fred ."

Blake looked very sorry to leave Fred, and so he was, too; but still he felt the truth of what Fred, said in its fullest extent, and he said not a word, although he shook hands with him and seemed deeply touched

" Courage," said Fred.

In another moment Fred had the spare horse by the bridle. for he meant to take it with him, in order that by its proximity to the cottage it might not lead his pursuers to think that it was there Jane had taken refuge, and off he went,

The horse he rode himself was of course now better able to make speed, for it was lightened by Jane, who, although no .great weight, was still something extra on a horse,s back, so that he was enabled to go at a gallop.

Fred's object was, the moment he got to any lane, to let the other horse go, and so get rid of it ; and he was not many minutes looking for such an opportunity before one presented itself to him. and he started the riderless horse off, and had the satisfaction of seeing it go at a canter right down the lane.

" That is all just as it should be ; and now," said Fred, " catch who may— catch who can. I will lead you a race for it at all events."

" Hilloa!" shouted a voice." hilloa!"

Fred did not slacken his speed, but he turned half round in his saddle, and to his surprise he saw his pursuers a good deal nearer to him than he had expected they could possibly be. It was quite clear that they had reached the high road by some near cut across the fields.

" The devil !" said Fred., " here they are."

" Hilloa !" cried the voice again. "Pull up, or we will fire at you—pull up. Hilloa !"

" Fire away !" said Fred, and he urged the horse on at increased speed, and with his light weight the powerful creature was able to get on tremendously. Bang ! went a pistol from the men in front, but it did no harm, and the probability is, that they only intended to frighten him by it, so as to induce him to stop. They did not know exactly, though, the sort of person they had to deal with. Fred was not of that order of beings that are easily frightened.

"Hold hard!" cried the voice again.

"On—on!" was all Fred said and on indeed he went at a rattling pace; but now a new danger came within sight. He saw one of those nuisances in the shape of toll-bars across the road. The man who presided at it evidently guessed that there was something amiss on the road, for he rushed out of his little cottage and shut the gate.

"I'll remember you for that another time," thought Fred.

A half minute more and Fred reached the gate, and over went the horse as if it had had wings.

"Murder!" said the man. "Stop him! It's three-pence."

"I'll call and pay you," said Fred.

Off he was again, but the gate was an obstacle to the pursuers, who were not so well mounted, or not so reckless as to what leaps they took, for they all stopped till the man opened the gate again, and his fright made him bungle so over doing it, that he delayed them nearly a minute.

"You idiot!" cried one of the officers, "if you had let the gate be we should have had him by now."

"But my three-pence, gentlemen—you know it's threepence. Look at the board with the list of tolls, if you please."

"Go to the devil!"

"Why, this is what you call a general bilk," said the toll-man. "I have been forced to let one fellow over the gate, and eight men through it, and I haven't got a penny piece from any of them. Oh, what a bilk!"

Fred had got considerably the start of his pursuers now, and really began to

think that there was a prospect of his escaping, when by the manner in which the horse began to go, he made the very uncomfortable discovery that he had turned lame. This was a circumstance that would have made any one else give up all hopes almost, but it had not that effect upon Fred, who was very far from belonging to the despairing class of human beings.

On the contrary, anything that happened to him of a very cross and perverse character, only had the effect of stimulating his intentions.

"What is to be done?" he said. "Why, I must forsake the horse, I suppose. He must have hit his heel against the top of that infernal toll-gate, and so is lame through it. I have promised to call again and pay that man, and won't I, that's all!"

To keep the high road now, and to lose ground every minute, was not exactly the wisest thing he could do, so he made up his mind to turn from it at the first opportunity that he possibly could; and seeing a lane to his right, he made a dash round the corner of it, and down went the horse on his knees.

There could be no doubt but that the creature had kept up as long as he possibly could.

Fred was thrown over its head very comfortably on the margin of a dung-heap, but he did not get hurt in the least, and was upon his feet in a minute.

Fred ran down the lane a little way, until through the hedge he saw a pretty garden, in which, close to the hedge, there was a quantity of scarlet beans growing with great luxuriance. He heard the clatter of the horse's feet of his pursuers. There was no time to choose what he should do, so he contrived to push his way through a gap in the hedge into the garden.

The little garden adjoined a cottage

that he could just see through the boughs of the fruit trees and over the tops of the beans and peas with which it was well stacked. Fred threw himself flat to the ground between two rows of peas, and then he heard the horsemen gallop past.

"Saved!" he said, as he got up.

Just as he spoke he heard the voice of a young girl in conversation with some one, and he crouched down again.

"I don't believe that he loves me," said the girl. "If he did, he could not behave as he does; and, at all events, as I don't love him, it makes no difference, and I will not see him."

"But, Mary," said another voice, which seemed that of an elderly woman, "I tell you that he is a very nice young man, and that his uncle is rich, and that you will ride in your own coach."

"I don't like coaches," said the girl.

"Money!" said the girl, when she was alone. "My aunt thinks of nothing but money, and the possession of that makes a lady, she thinks."

"She is quite wrong," said Fred, looking up. "Don't be alarmed, Mary. I would not harm you for the world."

"Oh, who are you?" said the girl, suppressing her tendency to scream for aid.

"A hunted hare," said Fred. "Don't you hear the hounds?"

CHAPTER V.

FRED MAKES AN APPEARANCE IN NEW-
GATE.

IT must have been the cheerful and kind tone in which Fearless Fred spoke, that assured the young girl that there was no danger to be apprehended from him; but she was rather puzzled at the odd manner in which he thought proper to let her know that he was pursued.

The girl was not above sixteen years of age, and she was very beautiful. Fred thought he had never seen such eyes, that had in them such a world of tenderness; but there was a delicacy of complexion, which, seemed to speak of fading health.

"Oh, tell me," she said, "who and what you are?"

"I am——"

Fred stopped short, for, to tell the truth, he did not know very well what to call himself to that young girl.

"Why do you not tell me who you are?" she said.

"Because I hardly know, and that's the real truth," said Fred in his pleasant and ingenuous way, that always had such a charm about it.

"But how can that be?" said the girl

"Easily. Nevertheless, will it not suffice if I tell you that there are no less than eight men on eight tailed horses in tent upon my capture or my destruction They will shoot me if they see me, and think they cannot capture me."

"Is that possible?"

"It is, indeed. Perhaps I deserve it, but yet I do not think so, for, after all, I feel as though I had been hurried on, by circumstances that I could not control, to do things the laws condemns I think you will save me if you can."

"Oh yes."

"Ah! I knew you would."

"I hope you are not very wicked?"

"Well, I don't think I am; but I am not very good, you may be sure."

"Come this way."

It was, indeed, time for Fred to go some way or other, for the horsemen had found Fred's horse, and not finding him, two of them had gone on for the full length of the lane, while the other six came back to see if he were hiding anywhere close at hand.

The beautiful young girl trembled very much as she ran along a little pathway, the sides of which were adorned with primroses, and then opening a rough-looking door at the end of it, she said—

"Go in there. It is where we keep the apples and other fruits that we want to preserve."

"Oh, but they will find me here."

"Not if you are careful. There is another door at the back of this little building, and if you hear them in the front here, you can leave it that way, and then come back again."

"I understand. And now, how can I thank you?"

"Not at all. I am afraid——"

"Of what?"

"That I am doing wrong."

"No. A kind action can never be wrong, Mary. You see, I know your dear, nice name, but if I didn't, I should never forget you, and I don't know why people are made with such pretty faces as yours, except to turn the whits of the rest of the world. Oh—"

Mary closed the door upon Fred, cut short his compliments; so that he was left to himself, and in comparative darkness, for although through a few crevices there did come little pencils of light, they were not sufficient to illuminate the place beyond the extent of a dubious kind of light.

"What a smell of apples there is here!" said Fred, as he stretched out his hand, and secured a fine one, which he began eating.

Fred had not got past the age when he could relish an apple with all the gusto of youth.

"Capital!" said Fred. "I feel myself very much refreshed; and if it were not that the image of Jane is at my heart, I should take it into my head that this Mary was the prettiest and gentlest creature in all the world; but, at all events, she is the next best, bless her!"

Fred thought, then, that it would be just as well to examine the mode of exit at the back of the apple house, and he found that it was a small door on the latch, which opened close to the margin of a little pond, upon which a couple of ducks were swimming.

"That will do," he said.

Any reflections or suppositions of Fred's were now put an end to by the actualities around him. It appeared that the officers had become so impressed with the belief that he must be hiding somewhere in the lane, or immediately contiguous to it, that they dismounted, and leaving their horses in the care of one of their number, they began hunting about the bushes at a great rate.

During their search they soon came upon the garden, and the idea struck them at once, from the rather dilapidated nature of the hedge, that he might have made his way through it.

"Here's a gap," cried one.

"It's too small," said another.

"Oh, I don't know; he is as thin as an eel; and, besides, the hedge can easily be pushed together a little on the inside, and he is cunning enough for that, I take it."

"No doubt about his cunning."

"Very well, then. You all of you keep a watch on this hedge, while we two go into the garden by the house way."

"Very good."

Thus was it, then, that two of the officers went to the front entrance to the cottage, and in the king's name demanded admittance. Mary's aunt was dreadfully alarmed; but she let the officers into the cottage, and thence into the garden at once.

"Oh, gentlemen," she said, "who is it you want?"

"A highwayman."

"Dear me! but there's no highwayman here, I assure you. I am not a highwayman, nor is my niece, Mary."

"We don't say you are, ma'am.; but your garden has not a very good hedge, and we suspect that the person we are after is concealed in it."

"In the hedge? Gracious!"

"No, in the garden."

Mary stood upon the little grass-plot in front of the cottage window and looked the picture of fright. Her face had turned quite white, and she trembled very much.

"You need'nt be afraid, my dear," said one of the officers. "We don't mean no harm to you."

"No—no, I am not afraid."

"That's right. But you look as if you had seen a ghost. You had better go in-doors."

"Why?"

"Because, you see, if we find the young spark we are after, there may be a little bit of a disturbance, for he is one that will crow and fight to the last, I know."

"But how cruel!"

"What is cruel?"

"Of you all, great big men as you are, to be pursuing such a mere lad."

"Ah! you have seen him. Do you hear that, Jarvis? This girl says he is only a mere lad."

"Does she so? That is capital! Now, my dear, all you have to do is just to say quietly where he is, and all will be right. By George, I thought he was here."

Poor Mary was ready to sink through the garden with remorse and terror at what she had said, for she now saw in a moment after the words had passed her lips what a testimony they had to strengthen their suspicions that Fred was hidden in the garden.

"Oh, no—no," she cried, as she clasped her hands. "I know nothing, indeed, I know nothing. I did not say I know anything, did I?"

"You did, though."

"Do not say that. Oh, aunt, what did I say?"

"Come on," cried the officer, as he drew a pistol from his pocket. "Come on—we shall unearth the fox, I rather think, pretty soon now. This way. Shoot him, so as to disable him if he should resist at all."

"All's right."

Poor Mary uttered a cry of despair, and sank upon her knees on the grass-plot. She had really wished to save Fred. There was a something in his looks which seemed so pitiable, and withal so frank and noble, that she could not believe he had done anything so very bad; but now she found that by her own indiscretion and want of tact she had destroyed him.

And yet what could she do now? Nothing but pray for him, and that she did most fervently.

Fred knew nothing of all this, as he was at a distant part of the garden; but if he had, he would have felt no indignation at that innocent girl, from whose very innocence and anxiety to do him good had arisen the words that were so much against him.

Poor, poor Mary—and poor Fred, too, for the matter of that, we may say, as he with all his faults, is to be pitied.

The officers had a sort of tact in searching the garden, although they would have searched a house better, as that was a thing they were more used to of the two; but still they did their work well, and they soon came to the little apple house.

Fred heard them.

"Now for it," he said. "I suppose my fate hangs upon the next five minutes."

"Here's a door," said one of the officers.

"Fire through it, then, if you can't open it," said the other.

"Oh, it's all right; it's only on the latch."

"What are you waiting for then, el?"

"Nothing—nothing, I only—that is, nothing."

The fact was, that the officer knew his danger, and that if Fred happened to be on the other side of that door, that in all true likelihood the salute that he would get from him would be a couple of bullets in his head. That idea was none of the most agreeable, and we do not at all wonder at the officer hesitating a little.

It was with a feeling of great relief that he called out when he opened the door—

"All's right."

"Not there?"

"No!" said the other one; "he is not there."

"What door is that at the back?"

"Let's open it."

"Ducce take your curiosity," thought Fred, and he tried to get very cautiously round the angle of the apple house, but his foot slipped and he half fell.

"Hilloa!" cried one of the officers, "I hear a noise."

"Take that, then," said Fred, as he fired a pistol at the head that popped out at the little door.

From the moment that Fred found that his presence in the garden was discovered, he felt that there was no possible chance for escape, and the shot he had fired was rather from impulse than from any reflection at all.

"Has he hit you, Ben?" cried the other officer.

"I don't know."

"That will do. Fearless Fred you are our prisoner. We are two to one here, and there are four more of us in the lane."

"I know it," said Fred. "Answer me one question."

"What is it?"

"Are you Peter Bayley's men?"

"We are not. We come from Bow street. My name is Jarvis. We have nothing to do with Peter Bayley."

"Upon what charge do you arrest me, then?"

"Highway robbery. You took a purse and a ring from a gentleman near Hendon. Now don't be a fool, Fred; we don't mean to take your life, but we must do our duty."

"All's right," said Fred. "If you had been Peter Bayley's men, I would have fought with you to the last gasp; but as it is, I give myself up to you, feeling that it would be just suicide to resist you."

"You have done a sensible thing, Fred."

"I hope so."

Fred walked very leisurely through the apple house, and confronted the two officers, to whom he handed his pistols.

"You ain't hurt?" he said to the one he had fired at.

"No."

"I am glad of that. It was a foolish and stray shot; but when one has a pistol in hand, and is taken by surprise, you know it is apt to go off."

"Just so. It's all in the way of business; only I wish my hat and wig had not gone into the duck-pond."

"So do I," said Fred.

At this moment Mary appeared, and clasping her hands, she cried—

"Oh, he is taken! They will kill him! He is taken!"

"Never mind," said Fred. "It's all right."

"But you are hurt. I heard fire-arms."

"No. Thank the fates no one is hurt; so there is no michief done ; and as for me, don't think ever again that you saw me. Forget me, Mary. Our acquaintance began this hour, and this hour let it end."

"I am very, very sorry for you."

"That I know ; and it's some consolation to feel that there is one kind heart that is sorry for me."

"I did all I could to save you."

"Hush !"

"Oh you did, did you ?" said one of the officers.

"Come on, now," said the other officer.

"Good-bye," said Fred, to Mary, and he held out his hand to her. She sprang towards him, and placed her little soft hand in his.

"Can you forgive me?" she said.

"Forgive you ? How ought I to thank you ! Hush ! The officers are not at hand now. Let me whisper to you. Have you a friend who will do a kind thing."

"Oh, yes, my cousin Phillip."

"The very thing. I——"

"Now, Fred ; come on."

"Let him go to Tottenham Cross to-night at twelve, and tell those whom he will see there what has happened to Fearless Fred. Do you comprehend me ?"

"I do."

The officer laid his hand upon Fred's arm.

"Come," he said, "I think you have said quite enough to the young lady now, Fred, and the sooner you come with me the better. I suppose you and she are old acquaintances ?"

"Not at all. I never saw her before to-day, and shall never see her again."

"Well, that is your look-out. She is a little beauty and no mistake. Come on."

There could be no doubt but that the officer had purposely held off to let him say a few words to Mary, with whom he believed that he was well acquainted, from the sympathy she showed for him.

In another minute they were outside the garden in the lane, and the officers began to mount their horses. The two who had gone up the lane now returned, and they were agreeably surprised to find that Fearless Fred was taken.

"Why, you really have him ?" they cried.

"Yes, all is right."

They mounted Fred behind one of them, and they then placed his hands behind his back, and put the handcuffs on him in that position, so that his chances of escape were really reduced to something very small, indeed ; but he did not contemplate escaping from those six men who had nothing to do but watch him.

"Tell me," he said, "if you can, and do your duty at the same time, how came you to be after me so quick ?"

"After what time ?" said one.

"Nothing," said Fred.

"Well, you have a right to be careful, Fred ; but the fact is, we thought you were dead."

"Ah, indeed !"

"Yes, Peter Bayley gave out that you were drowned in the river Brent ; but we met a lady in the road who told us that such a person as you, and she described you capitally, had taken her horse from her. We recognised the description at once, and though we were going on other business, we thought we could not do better than take you."

"That will do," said Fred. "Now, mind you, I don't care a straw about this arrest, provided you don't give me up to Peter Bayley."

Jane assailed by ruffians.

"That we are not likely to do. We hate the sight of him."

"So do I, and I have made up my mind to hang him."

"What?"

"I say I have made up my mind to hang Peter Bayley. Don't misunderstand me, I don't mean to hang him myself, but to get him hanged, in due course of law, for his crimes."

"If you can do that you are a clever fellow, Fred; but you forget that you are in rather a ticklish position yourself just now. Peter Bayley has all the evidence against you, cut and dry, in two or three cases of highway robbery."

"And yet I shall defeat him."

"Well, we shall see."

Fred was rather glad than otherwise that they did not take the road past the cottages near Stamford Hall, where Jane and Blake, and the young girl who had recently joined the party, were residing, for he did not wish to give Jane the shock of seeing him taken past a prisoner, although he hoped that Mary at the cottage would find some means of sending to Tottenham Cross, and so making the fearful fact known to her.

At the pace the officers went, London was very soon gained, and then they held a consultation with each other, and finally determined upon taking Fred before Sir John Rose, a magistrate who was always very severe against delinquents of his description.

The object of the officers, as Fred gathered from their conversation, was to get him sent to Newgate, for they did not think any other jail sufficiently safe to hold him, and they knew that, without an order from a magistrate, the authorities of Newgate would not take him in, as that prison was for offenders committed for trial, rather than for those who had not passed through that formality.

"It is quite a compliment," said Fred.

"What is a compliment?" said the officer who was upon the horse with him.

"Why, your wanting to take me to Newgate. Don't you think the new prison that is just built at Clerkenwell sufficiently strong?"

"No, I don't, indeed. The governor thinks more of his garden than of his prison, and there has been two escapes from there within the last week."

"Well, then, I take it to be very unkind of you, for you might as well have given a fellow a chance of getting away, but if you won't, why, you won't, that's all."

Sir John Rose was sitting at the old court in Bow Street, and in the course of ten minutes he heard enough from the officers to warrant him in specially remanding Fred to Newgate, where a ward was set apart for such specially remanded prisoners.

"You are young, said Sir John Ross, " but I regret to say, that I consider you to be a notorious criminal, and I have no doubt but that you will be hanged, which will be a very good thing for society at large."

"We differ very much in opinion, old pump," said Fred.

In another quarter of an hour, Fred was in the lobby of Newgate. A chill came over him, as he heard the door closed behind him

---

CHAPTER VI.

FRED. IN NEWGATE

We regret to leave Fred in such situation, but we are compelled to do while we pay just a little attention to Peter Bayley, and his manœuvres and operations.

That the box was in the old house somewhere Bayley still believed, and it was with something like an anticipation of getting it that he made his way to the house and knocked.

Peter was not the most patient of mortals, and when he found that no one replied to his knocking, he made such an appeal to the door, that it was enough to alarm the whole neighborhood.

Still no one came.

Peter Bayley then indulged himself in a few rather outrageous oaths, and it is to be supposed that they eased his mind a little, as he was rather more calm after them.

"The villain has gone to sleep," he muttered; "but I'll awaken him with a vengeance."

Peter then began upon the bell, but with no better effect than before; so he took from his pocket a skeleton key, with which he was always provided, and turned the lock of the door. It yielded in a moment, and Peter walked cautiously into the passage.

The naturally suspicious character of Peter Bayley made him always dread mischief to himself when anything of an unusual character occurred to him; and now that he found how quiet the house was, he would not go another step until he had got a pistol in each hand, and had loosened a knife in its sheath, which he wore concealed about him.

Then Peter stood in the passage, and called out loudly—

"Hilloa! hilloa, there!"

The dismal echo of his own voice up the staircase alone replied to him.

"It is very odd," said Bayley.

He remained silent now for some few moments, and bent his head down to listen, for he was in hopes that some slight noise in the house might yet be a guide to him, in case any one should be there.

All was as still as a grave.

"This is more than strange," added Bayley. "I will search the house; but first, I will provide against any surprise by the entrance to the house of any one else."

With this view, Peter put up the chain at the back of the street door, and shot a bolt into its socket; and then with his pistols still in his hands, he commenced his search through the premises.

Bayley proceeded to a thorough investigation of the house; but that afforded him no clue, and he returned to the parlor, more chagrined and enraged than ever.

"What can I do? What shall I do?" he said. "Baffled at every hand—my horse gone, and all the important papers that were in the pocket of the saddle—Jenkins false to me—and the cedar-box further off than ever! Curses!"

Here Peter indulged himself in a few more defamatory expressions touching mankind in general, and then he bounded out of the house, pulling the door shut after him with a loud noise.

We are glad enough to leave Peter Bayley, and turn to a consideration of more gentle and estimable natures.

We allude to Jane and the young girl who was with her, and likewise to Mary, the little beauty of the lone cottage in the lane, where Fearless Fred had had the evil fortune to be captured.

When Fred rode off at such speed, after leaving his dear friends at a cottage where they got, after all, but a frosty kind of reception—for the family were not at home, and an old sour-crabbed woman was only minding the place—they thought that he would be able to distance his pursuers and come back to them in an hour or so.

Jane pretended to be very much indisposed, in order to have an excuse to stay, and the servant could not very well turn her out, although it was evident she would have been very glad to do so; but when two hours had passed away, and no Fred came, Blake began to look rather grave, and to think in his own mind that something must have happened to Fred.

"Alas!" said Jane, in an under tone, for she had been watching the countenance of Blake, "alas! you dread the worst?"

"No no! All will be well."

"And yet your looks tell a different tale. You think that Fred is taken, or that he is dead, I know you do."

"Hush! do not speak so loud, I beg of you. We do not know who may be listening. Recollect that he told us to meet him at Tottenham Cross at midnight."

"Yes, yes!"

"Well, from that I gather the hope that he will be surely there, and that he may not think it prudent to come back upon this road, even though he may escape those who are pursuing him. He is much more likely to take to the many green lanes that lie to the west of Tottenham, and there hide until the night comes."

"Is that your real thought?"

"It is, indeed, Miss Jane."

"Then I will not despair while you, who ought to know these things as much better than I can, think there is room for hope."

It was very evident, indeed, that if they sought to stay where they were until the night came, they would out-stay their welcome; so, after a little more consultation, they decided upon giving up all idea of the return of Fred to the cottage, and to live upon the hope of meeting him at Tottenham Cross, to the immediate neighborhood of which they determined to repair.

With this resolve they left the cottage, after as coldly thanking the woman as she had been cold to them. Tottenham was by no means far distant from that spot. They had but to proceed down a green lane to find themselves in the High Street of that long, straggling suburb of the metropolis; and when there, they sought for the quietest looking inn, where they put up.

Now, all this time Jane had possession of the cedar-box, and knowing the great store that Fred set by it, she took the greatest care of it that could be. We will not go so far as to say that she had no curiosity regarding its contents, for Jane was human; and yet she did not think herself justified in opening the box without the presence of Fred. A kind of superstitious terror, too, clung to her as she looked at it, and she seemed to dread that its contents would be productive to her of more pain than pleasure.

"No, no," she said, "I will wait until midnight, and then I shall see Fred, and he will open the box."

To this determination Blake offered no objection. The behavior of this man now was so different to what one could at all have expected from one of Peter Bayley's satillites that it might well strike any one with astonishment, but the fact was, that the nature of Blake was good, and now that he found himself in the presence of goodness, and gentleness, and beauty, it altered all his feelings.

He, though, had his doubts about seeing Fred at Tottenham Cross at midnight.

And now, after long and weary waiting, the hour had nearly come when Jane and her friends might sally forth to keep that appointment with Fred, which, alas! he was so completely prevented from keeping with her. Little did she suspect that the gloomy walls of Newgate enclosed him at that time.

The night wind had risen in its strength, and, accompanied ny blustering echoes, was dashing about the tops of the tall trees. Now and then, too, a dash of rain came through the air; and afar off there was that continual moaning sound in the air, which in this country is so sure an indication of the continuance of rough weather.

Jane shrunk as she faced the cold night air, but Blake encouraged her to proceed, and shielded her as well as he could from the inclemency of the weather. He had all the hope in the world that Fred might be there, but he was quite prepared for a disappointment.

Tottenham Cross stood at that time in a much more secluded position than it does now, now that it is surrounded by houses, so that our friends could approach the spot without attracting much, if any observation, probably, at that still and solemn hour—a still and solemn hour in the sweet country, although in London at that time all the jarring elements of drunkenness and crime are let loose upon the face of society.

"He will surely be here," whispered Jane.

"Surely if he can," said Blake.

"But you do not doubt?"

"How can I doubt of a thing concerning which I can know nothing at all!

He said we were to meet him here; and setting aside the reverses, accidents, and circumstances that prevent people in this world from doing what they most wish to do, assuredly he will be there."

"Oh, yes — yes."

The tone in which Blake had spoken was quite sufficient to convince Jane that he had some doubts upon the subject, and she felt her heart sink within her as they all neared the cross, and no one came forward from it, as she knew that Fred would have come to meet them.

A dozen more steps and they stood by the cross. All was still. Jane felt as though she could have fainted upon the spot

"Oh, Fred, Fred!" she said, "where are you now? Fred, you are not here, and my mind sickens at the thought of what may be the cause of your absence."

"Did you say Fred?" said a voice, and at the same moment a figure emerged from behind the cross.

"Oh, speak to me—speak to me!" cried Jane. "Do you come from him?"

"From who?"

"Let me see you that I may be sure you are not an enemy. Let me look upon your face. The lantern, Blake, the lantern."

Blake had a small hand-lantern with him, which up to this time he had kept shrouded; but now he let a gleam of light escape from it, and it fell upon the ingenuous and pleasant looking face of a boy about sixteen years of age.

"My name is Philip," he said.

"But who are you? How came you here? Do you come from Fred?"

"No," said the boy, "it was my cousin Mary who told me to come here, and I always do what she tells me. She said I should meet some people here, to whom I was to say, that Fearless Fred was a prisoner."

"Oh, God!" said Jane, and she would have fallen, but that Blake supported her. She had dreaded and fully expected such intelligence as the lad brought to her; but still the realization of it was beyond her power to sustain with anything like firmness and composure.

"They have killed him!" she said. "Oh, they have killed him!"

"No, miss," said the boy, "there you are wrong. You may depend that such is not the case, or my cousin Mary would have told me as much. He is only taken prisoner by somebody."

"We thank you for being so kind as to bring us this information," said Blake. "Take back our kind acknowledgments to your cousin Mary, for taking so much trouble."

Poor Jane would fain have thanked Philip likewise, but she was in such a state of mental prostration, that she found it impossible to do so.

"Don't fancy," said Philip, "that I deserve any thanks. The fact is, I love my cousin Mary so well, that I always do whatever she tells me, and she says that Fred hid in their garden, and that she did all she could to save him, but could not."

"Blessings be upon her!" sobbed Jane.

"And so when he was taken," added Philip, "he asked her to send some one to this place at twelve o'clock with the news."

There was no more to be heard from Philip, and Blake bade him adieu, and turning to Jane, he said—

"It will be necessary now that you get to some place, as soon as possible, where you will be secure from Peter Bayley. I know an old couple who are taking care of a great farm-house that is to be let, at Wood Green, a little place close to Tottenham. There I can assure you of a welcome."

"Anywhere," said Jane, with a fresh burst of grief, "anywhere you please."

Blake led her to the place he had mentioned, where they knocked up the old couple, and where, from the kindness of the reception they got on Blake's account, it was quite evident that he had been of great service to them.

Blake told some portion of Jane's story to the old people, and then they offered to conduct her to her chamber, but she sobbed convulsively.

"All this will kill me," said Jane, "Do not, I beg of you, try to prevent me in any way from going to Fred. Surely they cannot be so barbarous as to wish to prevent any one from seeing him? Even the officers of the law cannot wish to heap more misery upon his head than he must suffer from the fact of his imprisonment?"

"You must not speak so, Miss Jane."

"And why must I not?"

"For several reasons. In the first place, if you attempt to go to Newgate to see Fearless Fred, you may certainly bring yourself into danger, but you can do him no good. You should recollect that the chief anxiety that he will suffer will be upon your account."

"That is true."

"And, therefore, I who know how to communicate with him, even though he were in the most gloomy cell of Newgate ought to be in a position to assure him with truth that all is well with you."

"Yes—yes. That is all true, likewise."

"Then you must abandon your idea of going to Newgate."

"I will," said Jane, as she sobbed convulsively. "I will."

Leaving, then, Jane and the other young girl to the care of Blake, we now return to Fearless Fred, who, it will be recollected, had just been taken into the lobby of Newgate by the officers.

CHAPTER VII.

RETURNS TO FRED IN NEWGATE

WE cannot pretend to say that even Fearless Fred, with all the natural courage of his disposition, felt nothing upon finding himself in that gloomy and terrible prison of Newgate. For the first time in his life a presentiment of evil fortune came over him.

The darkness of the lobby of the prison was too dark for the turnkeys even, who were used to it, to notice anything very particular, so they did not see the change of color that came over the face of Fearless Fred.

He, Fred, felt quite grateful to the darkness that prevented them from observing and commenting upon such a sign of weakness in him.

"The governor will be glad to see this new bird, who is going to make one in the old cage," said one of the officials of the prisoner.

'We won't give him up without the governor's receipt for him, I can tell you," said one of the officers who had brought Fred from the police office in Bow street.

"Oh, you will have your receipt, never fear. We do business, you see, in a business-like way, and so——"

"Hush!" said another. "Here is the governor coming, and one of the sheriffs with him. Stand back will you?"

The governor of Newgate was an old retired military officer, whose poverty more than his will had consented that the not very enviable post should be taken. He was a tolerable disciplinarian, though, and the only serious fault that he had, was a certain irritability of temper. which would peep out at times in a very undignified fashion.

The sheriff who accompanied him was a Scotch tailor, who, by dint of hard lying and spurious puffing, had made money, and so qualified himself for any civic office; and he was beginning a career which, he flattered himself, would end in the Lord Mayor's chair, by serving his first year of sheriffdom, if we may be allowed the expression with reference to that office.

"Noo, Mr. Governor," said the sheriff, "you will see, mon, the propriety of recommending to the authorities, which I cannot very well do mysel, that the turnkeys and such like should have the new great coats made by our house; and as you see, mon, it would no look weel for me to tak the order, why, my brother can do it for me, all being together, you understand, mon."

"I hope to Heaven you will, some day," said the governor.

"Eh, mon? What is that you say?"

"I said, I hoped you would."

"Oh, weel, I dare say it is some compliment to the way in which we do business, mon."

"Very well, sir. If you like to take it as a compliment, you may; but I beg to tell you, Mr. Tailor Sheriff, that I won't lend myself to your advertising tricks."

"Tricks, mon—tricks? Did you say tricks?"

"Yes, I did, so make the most of it. Now, Davis, do you want me for anything?"

"Yes, sir, if you please. Here is a special remand warrant from Sir John Ross."

"Oh, very well. I dare say Sir John Ross would not send any one here on a special remand, without good reason.

Who is it, I wonder? Hilloa! Fearless Fred! Is that the young fellow that Peter Bayley is so savage about?"

"Not a doubt of it," cried Fred "Peter, I think, would give one of his villanous ears to catch me; but I hope that I am in the hands of the proper authorities, and not of such a scoundrel."

"You are in Newgate, my fine fellow," said the governor.

"The governor of Newgate," said Fred, "is an officer and a gentleman, and he will do his duty. All I ask of him is to keep me out of the clutches of Peter Bayley.

"Peter Bayley has no more power here," said the governor, "than the man who sweeps the crossing at the corner of the Old Bailey"

"I am glad to hear it, sir. He pretends that he has power everywhere, and that he is superior to every one who is in any way connected with the administration of the law."

"Let him come here and try it," said the governor, drily.

"Fearless Fred, did you say?" cried the sheriff. "Did you say Fearless Fred was the youth's name, Mr. Governor?"

"Yes, I did, Mr. Sheriff."

The sheriff walked up to Fred, and looked at him from head to foot.

"And so you are the Fearless Fred that we have heard so much about lately? You are the gallant who has stopped me on the highway, are you? Who would have thought it!"

"There's your receipt, Mr. Davis," said the governor. "Sir John Ross may depend upon the safe keeping of this prisoner. Take him away!"

"Stop a bit," said the sheriff,—"stop. I just want to say something to the young man."

"This is very irregular," said the governor. "You should recollect, Mr.

Tailor Sheriff, that this is a prisoner, and that he ought not to be conferred with by any one."

"Tut—tut. man ! ain't I the sheriff? I won't detain him many minutes. Now, listen to me, young man."

"Go on," said Fred. "What is it?"

"You will be hanged."

"Well, so may you."

"God guide us, no! But never mind. I will excuse the expression. But I have a great favor to ask of you, and that is, that when you are hanged you will wear a coat that I will send you, and before you are turned off you will have the goodness to advance to the front of the scaffold, and say, "Good people, this coat was made by Messrs Tickell and Co., and it is the most comfortable coat a man can be hung in, and only one pound ten, cash price. Messrs Tickell and Co., merchant tailors. Many use the word snip, but they are the only true snips in London."

Fred looked at the sheriff, as he uttered with great volubility this harangue, which was a repetition of one of the sheriff's advertisements, and he thought surely the sheriff must be mad.

Fred little knew what the spirit of trading competition will induce people to do in London.

"Come—come," said the governor, "enough of this."

"Nay, but let me hear what he has to say to it," cried the sheriff; "surely if the young man can do me a favor and himself no harm, he will not refuse it. What do you say, Mr. Fred?"

"I say, that if anybody had told me what a heartless and brutal fool you were, I would not have believed it," said Fred; "and it only proves what a very small amount of intellect is required in trade in London. Don't trouble me, idiot!"

"Idiot! He calls me an idiot!"

"He is very wrong," said the governor.

"Oh, yes, very wrong."

"Yes," added the governor, in a whisper, "you are more rogue than fool. I would not pay you the compliment of calling you an idiot, for that would be to let you off some share of your awful selfishness."

"What do you say, governor?"

"Oh, nothing. I only said that, as a general thing, the world is rather selfish.

"That's uncommonly true," said the sheriff, with a sigh, "and it is wofully shown in the lad who won't do me a service though it will do him no harm Well—Well! Good-day, Mr Governor. I am going to see if I can't take off sixpence a week off the wages of the poor woman who make the waistcoats. They earn two shillings and eightpence already; and that's dreadful, for I hear that Abraham and Son only pay two-and-four-pence; so that I am getting swindled out of fourpence a week. Oh, gracious! it's awful to think of!"

"Confound that fellow!" muttered the governor when the sheriff was gone. "It is a disgrace to the City of London to pick up such men, and thrust them into office. Now, Fearless Fred, let me say a word to you."

"As many as you like, sir."

"As long as you are civil here, and make no attempt to give us the slip, recollect, that all the kindness that I can show you consistently with my duty, and all the indulgences that I can give you I will; but if you attempt any of your tricks, you had better be a cat in a certain place without claws."

"I hear you, sir."

"And do you understand me?"

"I think I do."

"Very good; that is all I have to say

to you. Put him in No. 40, Mr Green, if you please.;'

The governor turned upon his heel, and left the lobby.

" Is No 40 a very nice place, indeed ?" said Fearless Fred.

" Well, there's worse in Newgate said the officer.

" All's right, then. I shan't grumble But stop a bit; I have heard that the best thing a man can do when he gets here is to show that he thinks well of his jailers."

" Well, it isn't a bad thing."

" Very good. I have some money about me, but I want some of it for the support of those who are dependant upon me out of doors, as well as for the probable expenses of my own defence. If I halve with you what I have, will that content you ?"

" Quite, Fearless Fred. When a gentleman shows us that he is a gentleman, and wishes to act like one, we are never very particular what we do for him.".

" There's the money, then," said Fred ; " and all I can say is, that I wish it were ten times the amount, for all our sakes."

" All's right. You are a straight-forward sort of chap, and you won't lose anything by treating us in this sort of way, I can tell you."

" That he wou't," said the others.

Fred had heard quite sufficient of the mode in which affairs were conducted in Newgate to be well aware that, with the turnkeys and general officers of that prison, money was everything. All that is quite reformed now; but in Fearless Fred's time, if a prisoner was sent to Newgate and had plenty of money with him, so that he could fee the officers well in the shape of garnish, as they called it, he might do almost what he liked, with the exception of actually walking out of the gate into the street.

The cell marked 40 in which Fearless Fred was now in the course of a few minutes placed. was by no means one of the worst in the building. It was tolerably light, and was larger than the generality of cells. It was not an agreeable thing, though, for Fred to find that the governor thought proper to have a set of fetters placed upon him, for his better security.

" There's surely no need of these ?" said Fred.

" It's the governor's orders."

Those words were quite conclusive, and Fred felt how utterly useless it would be for him to raise any further objection to the fetters ; so, upon the principle which he had laid down for himself, of submitting with a good grace to everything that was unavoidable, he said not another word about the fetters.

One of the officers made a remark to the smith who was rivetting them on, and while the smith turned his head to reply, Fred took a file and a pair of pincers out of the basket of tools.

Luckily for Fred, no one noticed this rather daring act, or it would, no doubt, have been considered to be the commencement of hostilities between him and the authorites of the prison.

" Now, young fellow," said the smith, when he had finished his work, " get out of that if you can."

" Thank you," said Fred.

" Oh, he don't want to get out." said an officer. " He is all right enough, and from what I can hear, I don't know that it will go very hard with him on his trial, either"'

" Peter Bayley is my enemy," said Fred.

The officer whistled.

" Oh, well, if that's the case, he has made up his mind about you, one way or the other. He will bring you through the affair altogether as neat as possible or he will hang you."

" Or he will neither," said Fred.

" Well, you know your own business best, young gentleman I wish you luck that's all. I rather like you than not Poor Fred had managed to keep up his spirits pretty well while he was in the presence of the officers, but when he was quite alone, he found himself quite overwhelmed at the idea that at last he was an inhabitant of that gloomy prison, which always had risen up before his imagination full of sadness and terror. He began to compare his present condition with that time when his father lived, and whatever might have but been the evils and discomforts of his position, in consequence of Mrs. Martindale, he was, at least, innocent of crime.

From these reflections, then, Fred passed on to a dearer one—of his first meeting Jane, and the singular manner in which she had been thrown upon his precarious protection; and then he asked himself what would become of her if he should be cast for death, and not be able to escape the doom which the law then with a much greater amount of recklessness then now, dealt out even to those who had committed only crimes against property.

Other offences, though, could easily be brought to bear against poor Fred, for when he had been attacked, we know that he had not been over-scrupulous in the way in which he defended himself. From these thoughts he brought his reflections right down to his present position; and then when he began to consider his age, and how much he had gone through, he thought it was hard to die yet.

He lean his head upon his hand, and gave himself up for an hour or more to those frightful reflections, and they might have lasted longer but that he heard the clank of footsteps upon the stone pavement outside his cell, and then the rattle of the chains and the heavy fall of the bar that secured the door.

" Hilloa, Fred !" said a voice.

" Who is that ?" said Fred.

" All s right; only a visitor, that's all. Walk in, sir ; you will find him there." Who is it?" cried Fred.

The cell was quite dark, for it was evening time now, and in that gloomy place the daylight had but to half go to produced a complete night in the atmosphere, so that all Fred could see was a dark figure crossing the threshold of the cell. That figure, though, had a lantern with him, with a slide to it that shut up or exposed the light of it at pleasure, and now, when the door of the cell was closed, the visitor moved the slide of the lantern back with a sharp crack, and holding it up, let the bright beam of light all upon his face.

" Peter Bayley! " said Fred.

" Ha ! ha !" said Peter.

" I thought that I was, at least, free from you here," added Fred. " I don't know what right you have to come troubling me. I will not speak with you "

Ha ! ha !" laughed Bayley in his odd manner, again, " you won't speak to me ?"

" No, you infernal scoundrel, I won't except to tell you what I think of you."

" Have a care, Fearless Fred. Keep civil. Your fate is in my hands. Do not tamper with your life."

" I don't believe it !"

" Well—well, we shall see. I came here by virtue of an order from the Secretary of State, which will admit me at all times and at any time I like to your cell. You cannot shake me off, Fearless Fred. I have made a determination to stick to you now while you live."

Fred made him no answer.

FEARLESS FRED.

"And now," added Peter, "I begin to believe in the truth of the old saying, that if a man is born to be hanged, you can't drown him."

Fred knew that Peter alluded to the affair at the river Brent, when he, Fred, had gone off upon Bayley's horse, for Peter was by no means as yet possessed of the particulars of that affair. Still Fred made him no sort of answer.

"You may speak or not," added Bayley. "I have come to you to say my say, and when I have done I will leave you to think it over. Your life, I tell you, Fearless Fred, is in my hands. It is in my power to manage to soften or to aggravate the evidence against you in the cases of highway robbery that will be brought forward against you, so as to insure your acquittal or your conviction. If you are convicted, nothing on earth can save you from the gallows."

"What means?" said Fred.

"Oh, you have found your tongue? Well, Fred, I am a man who is very much misunderstood. Some folks think I bear malice."

"Oh!" said Fred.

"But I don't—oh, dear, no. There is a peculiarity in my disposition that enables me always to forgive those things that seem to be the most directed against me from a brave man. I say, that is one of my little peculiarities."

"I have heard," said Fred, "that you have a few."

Fred felt quite certain that Peter Bayley had some deep design in visiting him in this way, and his curiosity was aroused to discover what it was; so he was tempted to forego his first resolve not to speak to him at all.

"Yes," added Bayley, as he placed the lantern upon the little wooden table that constituted, beside the truckle bed, the only article of furniture in the cell,

"yes, Fearless Fred, although you have aimed more than once at my life, I can yet forgive you."

"Your virtue," said Fred, "is quite wonderful."

"Sneer away—sneer away, Fearless Fred; I give you, young as you are, credit for more active good sense than many who are double your age; and so I have a direct and clear offer to make to you, upon your acceptance of which you may save your life."

"Go on, Peter!"

"There is a little cedar box——"

"Oh, are you there, Peter! There certainly is a little cedar-box. Well, what of it?"

Bayley was rather agitated, and generally calm and cool and collected as he was, he found a difficulty to repress the feelings of impatience that possessed him; but he spoke slowly, notwithstanding, although the couched tone of his voice sufficiently betrayed the inward workings of his spirit.

"I tell you, then, Fearless Fred, that if you will place that cedar-box in my hands, I will guarantee you your life."

"Oh, indeed! It's only the box you want?"

"Pshaw! The contents of course."

"Well, Peter, it is a fair enough offer."

"It is such a one as only I can make you. I have the power to save you, and not only will I do it in this instance, but I will for the future hold my protecting hand over you, and the lock of a prison shall never again turn upon you, nor a felon's fetters gall your limbs."

"Umph!"

"You doubt my power? That is foolish, Fred. I tell you that it is competent for all that I promise. The administration of the criminal law in this country is so loose, that any bold, enter prising man could step in and exercise a power just in proportion to his unscrupulousness. You see, I don't pick my words when I am talking to you. Fred, because I wish that you should plainly understand me. I am such a man, and by one means and another I have great power either for life or for death. I can save you, or I can destroy you. Which shall it be? I pause for your answer, Fearless Fred."

"You shall have it."

"The box?"

"Oh, no! My answer I meant."

"Don't play with your existence in this way, Fearless Fred. You are young enough to wish to live, surely?"

"Yes, I own that I wish to live, but there are considerations superior even to the wish to live. It is true—quite true that I know where to lay my hand upon that box you speak of."

"You—you do—you do, Fred?"

"I do, Peter."

"Then you will tell me at once. good Fred. You are not so mad as quite to throw your life away for a foolish cedar-box. Oh, no—no! Where is it? Speak, Fred, and make me your friend for ever."

"That is something!"

"It is everything to you, Fred—it is life instead of death—it is daylight instead of darkness—it is the world instead of the grave!"

"Oh, yes, I know all that. Well, then, Peter, you won't let it go any further?"

"No—no, good God no!"

"You won't be angry—you won't breathe the secret to any one else even in the strictest confidence?"

"No, I say; a thousand times, no!"

"Well, then, Peter, the box is—that is to say, the cedar-box tied up with a piece of red tape, found by me in Lolanti's house——"

"Go on! D——n, why do you play with me in this way."

"I play with you? I play with the great Peter Bayley? You might as well ask a mouse to play with a cat. I tell you, therefore, frankly and freely, Peter Bayley, that the cedar-box with the red tape around it, about eight inches long and about four in width, that I found in Lolanti's house after the death of that personage"

"Gracious Heavens! Yes—yes."

"Well, listen: If these were the last words I had to speak in this world, they should be as true. The box is—"

"Well?"

"You are sure that turnkey ain't listening at the door?"

"D——n it—no?"

"Then, it is in a very safe place."

"Well?"

"Well, I say, it is in a very safe place. What would you have more?"

"But where is it?" cried Peter, in a thundering voice of rage.

"That is a little piece of information," said Fred, calmly, "that I mean to keep to myself: and if every hair on your head, Peter, was a diamond, and you were to shave them all off and offer them to me, I would not tell you!"

Bayley raised his hand to strike at Fred, but the latter sprang to the table, and seizing the lantern, he flung it in Peter's face, and out it went, leaving the cell in the most profound darkness

"Help! Help! Lights! Hilloa! Turnkey!" cried Bayley. "Open the door. will you!"

"Hoi! what's the row, now?" said the turnkey, opening the door of the cell, and holding up his lantern.

"He tried to murder me," said Bayley.

The turnkey grinned, as he looked at Fred sitting very composedly on his bed, while Peter Bayley had a large pistol in his hand.

"Why, Mr. Bayley," said the man, "one would have thought that you might have taken care of yourself from such a boy as that, with fetters on his limbs, too. You must be joking, Mr. Bayley."

"No—no," said Bayley, " my feelings were overcome. I was talking to him about—about his poor mother, and offering to protect him. He has broken her heart, poor woman. He is a most hardened criminal."

"Really," said the officer.

Peter Bayley turned his frightfully ugly countenance towards Fred, and in a voice almost inarticulate with rage, he said—

" Remember me !"

" Easily," said Fred ; " you are so infernally ugly, that, once seen, it is quite impossible for any one to forget you."

The turnkey burst into a loud laugh, for, after all, they did not care much for Peter at Newgate.

" Ay," said Bayley "laugh now, I like to hear it ; but when I say that I will change the laugh of every man to groans, I generally—mind you, I say I generally keep my word. Good evening, Fearless Fred—good evening, Mr. John Holmes, under-turnkey at Newgate. Good evening, and very pleasant dreams to both of you."

The turnkey looked a little alarmed, for well he knew that when Peter Bayley determined to be spiteful, he would stir heaven and earth to be so ; but, after all, he thought, what could Bayley do to him ?

"I don't know, Mr. Bayley," he said " what harm there is in our laughing. It ain't quite the most cheerful place in the world, this Newgate."

Fred was more troubled at this visit from Peter than he chose to let that villian see ; but yet he was, upon reflection

something of the opinion of the turnkey, namely, that Peter could not do him much injury, after all. That he would be put upon his trial for highway robbery, looked beyond a doubt, and that if the witnesses chose to depose to the facts, he would be executed, was likewise pretty clear ; but beyond that the danger ended. That is to say, ended with his existence, for in those days, to be committed was to be hung.

" I should like to live," said Fred, " for the sake of Jane. Bless her, how desolate she will be without me ; and when I am no more, she ——. Pshaw ! I will not have such gloomy thoughts— I will not yield even to the despondency of such a situation as mine. I will hope to the last. Ah ! the file and pincers that I took from the smith's basket—I had well-nigh forgotten them. What can I do with them ? I have heard of men making their way to freedom with worse implements than a file and a pair of iron pincers."

Fred groped about in his dark cell till he laid hands upon both his tools, and then the idea occurred to him that in the morning he would be certainly taken before Sir John Ross to be formally committed for trial, and that if he were to tamper with his fetters then it would be surely found out, whereas, after his committal he would have ample time to think of what was best to be done, pending the day of his trial. Under these circumstances, Fred adopted a wise course.

" I will hide these tools," he said : " they are of no use to me now, but they may be another day."

With this resolve, he managed to hide the file and the fincers in the mattress that was given him to sleep upon, and then, such a feeling of weariness came over Fred that he gave in to the opinion, that let a man's situation be what it may, and let his anxieties be of what sort or complexion they may, sleep he must.

"I would pray for Jane," he said, as he flung himself upon the hard mattress, "but I am afraid I am not innocent enough to pray. God will protect her without any prayers from me.'

For all this, though, Fred, before he closed his eyes in sleep, uttered with deep sincerity the words—

"God bless her!"

This was a very good prayer, and quite enough.

It seemed to Fearless Fred as if he had only slept for a few minutes, before he felt himself rudely shaken by the shoulder, and a rough voice cried—

"Up—up, and be stiring, Fearless Fred. We don't lie in bed late of a morning here."

Fred started to his feet.

"What's the matter?" he said.

"The matter? Oh, nothing particular is the matter, only, old fellow, you will be wanted to go before the beak, you see."

"Why, it's daylight!"

"Daylight? Of course it is. Did you think, because you were clapped up in the stone-jug, that the daylight was never to come again, eh? What an idea!"

"No," said Fred, "I did not think that, but I slept so sound that the night has passed away like nothing at all. But I am all right now. Breakfast, if you please, for I am rather inclined that way."

"Well, you can have the prison fare, and that is gruel and a bit of not the softest nor the whitest bread; but if you like to pay, why, you can have—"

"Anything I like, I suppose?"

"Exactly."

"Take that guinea and get me as good a breakfast as your conscience will let you, and keep the change."

"You are a trump, Fearless Fred, and no sort of a mistake. I will do you justice, you may depend; and if I don't spend half of it upon you, call me a Frenchman."

Fred had, in the course of a quarter of an hour, an excellent breakfast laid before him, which was got from a neighboring tavern; and being so fortified against any suffering from hunger, he was pretty well prepared for the events of the day. About ten o'clock he was conveyed in a hackney-coach to Bow street, and introduced to the sitting magistrate, who seemed inclined to make short work of the affair.

Fred had fully expected that Peter Bayley would make an appearance at the court, and bring forward what evidence he could against him, but in that he was mistaken, for Peter did not make his appearance. It was one of the gentlemen who had been attacked by Fred in the early part of his career, and from whom he had taken a purse of money, who appeared and distinctly swore to him. The charge was so clear, that the magistrate turned at once to Fred, and said—

"Have you anything to say?—I suppose not!"

"You seem in a great hurry," said Fred; "surely it is not dinner-time yet?"

This produced a laugh in the court, for his worship was rather notorious for knocking off the cases when the hour for his refreshment arrived, although Fred did not know that; so it was upon his part, quite an accidental hit.

"How dare you address such an observation to the bench?" said the magistrate. "Any one would think that you meant to intimate that we preferred our dinners to our duty." The officers and clerk of the court shook their heads with horror at any such supposition. Alas! what hypocrisy there is in this world!

"Well," said Fred, "perhaps it's only lunch that you were thinking of, so I won't detain you any longer; you can do just as you please in this matter, and I don't take any merit to myself for allowing you to do so, since I know you will do it, whether I give you leave or not.

"You stand in a very serious situation, indeed, young man," said the magistrate, shaking his head, "and I am sorry to see that there is in your conduct a kind of levity, which shows that you are anything but perfectly alive to the peril of your situation."

"Thank you," said Fred.

"You stand committed for trial upon the direst charge; and let me tell you, that there are several others against you, if this should by any accident fail."

"Oh, don't trouble yourself. You are too good by half. Don't you fret yourself about me, or you won't be able to eat that lunch you seem so anxious about, you know."

"Take him away," said the magistrate; "I perceive that, young as this Fearless Fred is, that he is a most hardened criminal. Nothing shows a thoroughly depraved disposition so much, as a want of reverence for those in authority."

Fred was reconducted to Newgate; and as he went in the coach with the officer, that personage said to him—

"Fearless Fred, I have been offered a couple of guineas to give you a note, but I don't think I ought to do it."

"Oh, yes, you ought," said Fred, "for you are a good fellow, and you know that it will never be known to any one who could injure you in consequence;

and you know, too, that I will give you a couple more to give it me at once."

"Well, I like to do a kind action when I can; and as far as I am concerned, Fred, I don't think you one half so bad as Peter would fain make you out."

"Not a quarter. But how do you know that Bayley has been trying to make me out bad?"

"Oh, he was with the magistrate for half an hour in his private room, before you were brought to the office."

"Indeed! The villain! But I won't vex myself about him. I expected from the first every hostility that could be brought to bear against me on his account; so give me the letter you say you have."

The officer handed a little note to Fred, who eagerly opened it, and read the following lines:

"Keep good courage; J. is quite safe, and in a place of security. I will do all I dare do to aid you; and what I dare do, will be only transcended by my ardent wish not to leave J. utterly friendless.

Fred understood very well that this note came from Blake, by the signature J. to it, and that by J. he meant Jane. It was a great consolation to him to feel such an assurance as the note gave him; and, although he did not think it possible that Blake could aid him in any way, yet that he would try to do so kept him from utterly despairing of his situation and prospects.

Fred was in some anxiety now lest, having been duly committed for trial, he should not be conveyed to the same cell, for there he had hidden the file and the pincers, which he regretted he had not taken with him; but he soon got rid of the apprehension that his place of confinement would be changed, for he was conducted direct to the same cell, and there left. When he was alone, he sat down and began to think over his situation and prospects, and, to tell the truth, they were sufficiently gloomy to have struck terror into any bosom. The Old Bailey sessions would be on in a very few days, and he felt pretty confident that he would be got rid of as quickly as possible. Peter Bayley would take good care that such was the case.

"Yes," said Fred, as he rose, and paced the narrow dimensions of his cell, "Yes. That villain, although, perhaps, he may not have it in his power to exercise any direct influence over the judges of the land, can yet do much to expedite the fate of any one against whom he has such an enmity as he has against me. Perhaps, after all, it would have been wiser to temporise with him than to defy him as I have done. Ah, Jane, I do not like to leave you yet."

"Save her, then, and yourself," said a voice, and then Fred found that the cell door had been all but opened, and that some one was listening to the thoughts that Fred gave expression to in words from his lips in what he thought the solitude of his cell.

"Who speaks?" said Fred; "surely it is the poorest privilege that a prisoner can ask to be alone."

"We don't give prisoners privileges," said Peter Bayley, stepping into the cell at once, and confronting Fred.

"Oh, it is you, devil, is it?"

"Yes. it is. You can call me what you please. Fearless Fred; I always accede to a man who has his fetters on the privilege of saying what he likes. It is to be expected that his temper should suffer a little. If you were to sneer a little now, Fearless Fred you would feel all the better afterwards, I am certain."

"I don't want your advice, Peter Bayley. Why do you persecute me?"

"Persecute you? Oh, dear, no. That is quite a mistake Fred. I rather love you than otherwise. You are a man after my own heart; and now that you are committed for trial, I am here, you see, still to offer you hope."

"Well?"

"That cedar-box, Fred."

Fred turned full upon Peter, and looked him full in the face.

"I am glad you are come, Bayley," he said, "for I had something to say to you that I did not say last night when I saw you. Now, listen to me: The cedar box, and the papers that were in the little pocket under the flap of your saddle——"

"D——n!" said Bayley. "Have you them, too?"

"Oh, yes, all safe. But do not lose your temper, Peter; recollect that you have not fetters upon your limbs, although the time will come when you will have such, you may be assured. But don't put yourself in a passion. The cedar-box and the papers that were in your saddle-pocket are in the possession of one who will religiously keep them without even looking at them."

"Ah, indeed!"

"Unless he hears of my death: then he will carefully examine them and take them to such persons in authority as he may think will act with vigor in the matters that they relate to."

Peter's very lips turned white.

"You are joking, Fearless Fred," he said, "you are like a child who plays with edge-tools; you don't know your own danger."

"Very good!"

"I tell you, you don't know what that box contains——eh?"

"Very good!"

"Villain! Have you dared to read documents that cannot concern you, and the knowledge of which is sufficient of itself to make your death a thing to be desired ?"

" Go on, Peter !"

" But—but, Fred, you are yet young —you are under twenty—you cannot pretend to mean but that life is sweett you. Do not tell me that already you have seen enough of life to care little for it. I can save you, if you will let me do so. Ah, who comes here ?"

———

CHAPTER VIII

PETER BAYLEY DOES WHAT HE CAN
FOR FRED.

THE tone of voice in which Peter Bayley expressed his surprise at the approach of any one at the door of the cell, was very well acted indeed, and seemed extremely natural ; but yet Fred could not but have the idea at the moment that it was a piece of acting, and he was determined to be upon his guard accordingly.

The cell door was flung open by the turnkey rather ostentatiously, and he cried out—

" Here's more company for you, Fred."

" I don't want any more company," said Fred ; " that which I have is more than is agreeable."

The stranger was a tall, bulky, heavy-browed looking man, and the moment he cast eyes upon Peter Bayley, he said—

" Who is this ? Turnkey ! Hilloa there ! I thought this youth, in whose fate I chose to interest myself, was alone ? Who is this man ?"

" Why, sir," said the turnkey, " that is Mr. Peter Bayley "

" Peter Bayley ? What, the notorious Peter Bayley !"

" The same, sir."

" Then I shall certainly decline remaining here in the presence of such a man. I will endeavor to call some other time."

" Oh, don't mind me," said Bayley, " I am going : though I don't know what objection you can have to me, seeing that I never saw you in my like before."

" But, sir," cried the portly man, " I have heard of you, and I do not desire to have anything to say to you. If you are going, go at once ; I came here on a mission of kindness and benevolence to this lad here, who, I presume, is Fearless Fred, and I do not choose to be mixed up in any proceedings of yours."

" Oh, well, I'm off ; but you might be civil, whoever you are. That you are a gentleman, and have power to do a good deal for Fearless Fred, if you like, I dare say ; but you need not be so uncivil to me ; for all that, notwithstanding."

There was something so uncommonly artificial in all this, that Fred was much too acute to be deceived by it. The last speech of Bayley was so unlike a reproach to the portly man, that it at once was convincing to Fred that something in the shape of trickery was going on.

Bayley walked out of the cell, putting on the look of a very much injured and insulted man, and then the portly stranger called out in a voice of authority—

" Turnkey, close the door, and do not let me be interrupted in what I have to say to this unfortunate young man."

" All's right sir," said the turnkey and he closed the door of the cell ; but although Fred listened attentively, he did not hear him fasten it, and a strange idea came over him that Bayley was there listening to what should take place between him and the portly man.

" And so. your name is Fearless Fred " said the unknown visitor.

"Yes," said Fred. "What is yours?"

"Oh, my lad, you must not be so inquisitive I hope to entitle myself to your gratitude, and then you shall know all. Suffice it to say, that I am a member of parliament, and that I can be of good service to you. The fact is, that your case came under discussion last evening between me and one of the cabinet ministers, and I said, that I lamented very much that a lad of your age, who I had heard was educated, should die the death of a felon for a few indiscretions; and his lordship agreed with me; so that, in fact, after a time, it was agreed that I should call upon you, and learn your entire history from your own lips, and then draw my own conclusions from it."

"How very kind!" said Fred.

"Oh, no—no. Not much. But never mind that. It is a hard case if we who have rank, and wealth, and influence, may not enjoy the pleasure of doing good sometimes."

"A very hard case indeed," said Fred

"Well—well, now for your history. You will be so good as to tell me who and what you are, and everything of importance that has happened to you, and I wish to know if you have any friends, or if any particular anxieties press upon your mind in any way, in order that I may alleviate them all. I was sorry to see Peter Bayley with you, for I am afraid he is a bad man."

"So am I," said Fred.

"Well, never mind him—I will protect you against him. Let me hear your history."

"It must be very interesting," said Fred, "but you shall hear it. My father, then, you must know, was the husband of my mother He was a human being, and had his faults and good qualities like most people; and as for my mother, they used to say that when she was young she looked youthful."

"Well—well, pass over all that."

"Very good. I was brought up principally upon victuals and drink, and had the measles at the interesting age of five. On the following morning after the first appearance of that melancholy disease——"

"Well, pass that."

'Very good. I don't think anything worth the telling since I had the measles, till they brought me here, and accused me of highway robbery; so now, sir, you know it all."

The stranger bit his lips and looked angry; but he passed it off with a smile, and then said—

"Come—come, Fred, you are a wit, I see, and will yet make a figure in the world. Believe me, my good young man, that I am very happy to make your acquaintance, indeed, and that I will do everything I can for you. But now be candid. Is there no one dependant upon you, towards whom I and my lady could extend the hand of kindness, Why, such a good looking young fellow as you ought to be in love by this time. Is there no charming and innocent young creature, that the hand of kindness might be extended to? Only tell me the particulars, and my wife shall see to her at once."

This speech confirmed Fred in the suspicion that had been gaining upon him from the commencement of the interview, namely, that the portly individual was no other than the earl, who had taken so active a part, along with his unprincipled lady, in the persecutions of Jane. That this rascally individual had now, at the instigation of Peter Bayley, come to him under the mask of sympathy to try to get from him the particulars that would again enable him to seize up

on Jane, seemed but too probable. Indignation prompted Fred to say some
thing of a passionate character, but by a
strong effort he controlled the impulse
so to do.

He shook his head.

"No—no. I am surprised, sir, that
you should wish a person in my situation
to fall in love."

"I don't wish it, only I thought it was
likely enough, the more especially as you
are a well-looking lad enough."

"Quite a mistake, sir. I have told
you all."

"You doubt my power to be of service
to you, That is foolish and ungeneral,
Fred. You will never make friends if
you give way to such feelings of suspicion. To reassure you at once, I tell you
that I am a nobleman."

"Well, if I did'nt think so," said Fred.
"But a word in your ear, Mr Nobleman;
I don't mean to tell you where Jane is,
for all that."

"Confusion!"

"Curses!" cried Peter Bayley, pop-
ping his ugly head in at the door of the
cell.

"Ha—ha!" laughed Fred. "It is
confusion and curses now, is it? Well
—well, you see it is a failure, both of you,
except so far, my lord, that I have had a
good look at you now and am not likely,
to forget you again in a hurry. You,
and your dear friend, Peter Bayley, may
leave me now, with the conviction that
even to death, I will hug my secret to
my bosom."

"You shall die!" said the earl.

"Perhaps I shall; but if I do, there
will rise up yet friends for Jane, who
will fight for her as I have done; and
the day will come when you, my lord,
and your infamous countess and all your
confederates, will be grovelling in the
dust."

"Strike him, Bayley! Knock him
down!" said the earl.

"Oh, no," said Bayley, "but I will
hang him in ten days from now, my lord.
to a certainty."

"No you won't," said Fred.

"Indeed, won't I! I tell you what
it it, Fred—you are a great deal too
clever to live long, and I will wager one
of my ears that I get you hanged."

"Done!" said Fred.

"Ha, ha!" laughed Bayley, faintly.
"That will do. Done, then; a twist of
the neck to you, Fred, or one of my ears.
Done be it. I have strung up many a
fellow for looking awry at me, and it isn't
likely I am going to fail now, is it, my
lord?"

"Fred," said the earl, advancing in an
agitated manner, "before I leave you, I
make you one proposal."

"It is useless, my lord," cried Bayley,
"it will do mischief"

"No—no, Bayley, surely he cannot be
so deaf to all the advantages that I can
offer him. He is human. Listen to me,
Fred: if you will tell me where I can
find Jane, and the little cedar-box that
was hidden in Lolanti's house, I will not
only save you from the gallows, but, I
will give you a large sum of money, and
you may take Jane abroad and marry
her at once, if you like, and I will always
keep you both above want as long as you
live."

"When I see Jane again," said Fred
"I will mention it to her."

"See her you never will, unless you
embrace my offer. Will you write to
her, and act upon her answer?"

"No."

"No? What do you mean by this
obstinacy? You ought to write to her
and let her decide."

"Perhaps I would," said Fred, "but

The earl made no reply; and Peter Bayley; with a look of mingled hatred and anticipative triumph, at the prisoner, preceded the portly nobleman in his exit from the cell.

"Not caught in that trap!" muttered Fearless Fred, as the iron door closed upon his visitors. And now, as all their cunning and influence will of course be used to ensure my destruction, I must turn my thoughts to my escape."

A few moments of reflection satisfied the intelligent tyro that his efforts for freedom could only be made with safety during the night. And he therefore sighed for the departure of the day.

"In the meantime," he murmured, "it will be good policy to relieve my wrists and legs of these ugly-looking manacles.

No sooner said, than done. Drawing forth from their hiding-place, his file and pincers, he applied himself to the delightful task of ridding himself of his chains. His progress was necessarily very slow; but, as he was fortunately uninterrupted during the day, he succeeded by nightfall in not only filing off his chains, but also in removing one of the seven iron bars which belonged to the window of his cell. About ten o'clock, he took up his iron bar, and commenced prying out a large stone in the wall opposite the door of his cell. The bar soon removed the cement on the outer part, and in less than an hour thereafter, he succeeded in loosening the stone, which he was shortly enabled to remove altogether from the wall. But his work was not yet finished; for as he looked into the space which had been created by the withdrawal of the stone, Fred heard the sound of an iron instrument striking against the wall on the other side. Surprised he held his breath and listened. The noise, though occasionally interrupted, still continued. Fred reflected.

"It is possible," he murmured, "that the sound is occasioned by some prisoner, who, like myself is endeavoring to escape!"

This surmise eventually proved correct. In an hour or so, a stone was carefully withdrawn from the inner wall, and a head peered through the open space.

"Holloa!" cried Fearless Fred. "Who are you?"

"I'll take the liberty of putting the same question to you!" was the answer, although in a somewhat disconcerted voice.

"I am Fearless Fred, the Highwayman!"

"And I am Ned Jacks, the Housebreaker. What are you up to that I find this hole in your wall?"

"You might easily answer that interrogatory yourself," replied Fred. "When a prisoner makes a space like that in either of the walls of his cell, it can be but for one object."

"True," returned the housebreaker. "We understand each other. And now, as we have no time to lose, I will take the liberty of paying you a visit."

So saying, Jacks crept through the hole in the wall, into the young highway man's cell.

"I thought," he said, "when I was working away at the wall, that there was no one in here."

"And I thought, when working on my side of the wall that there was a passage on the other side of it," said Fred.

"No," observed Jacks, "the passage is

on the other side of your door. And the best thing we can do is to reach it at once."

"How!"

"I'll show you," replied Jacks, "when I have struck a light."

The housebreaker appeared to be fully provided with everything needful for one in his position. Taking a tinder-box from his breast, he struck a light, which he applied to the wick of a small night lamp which was scarcely larger than a man's thumb. Then running his hand through his thick, bushy hair, he, to Fred's astonishment, drew out a skeleton-key, with which he soon turned back the lock. Then, with Fred's small iron bar, he forced out the bolts which sustained the hinges, and in another moment the door stood open.

The passage into which the cell opened, was paved with flat flag-stones, and Fred was rather surprised that it was not guarded by a turnkey; but it was not, so they had nothing to do but to traverse it to the end; but there they were stopped by a closed door.

"Through this door," said Jacks, "is a yard."

"What are we to do next!" asked Fred.

"Open this door, to be sure. It is rather clumsy than strong, I take it, and I daresay, after all, it is only locked. I will try it with my skeleton-key, although, I am afraid, it is too small for the lock."

The housebreaker made a dozen fruitless attempts to catch the lock with the skeleton-key, but it as often slipped past it. At length, he roughed the key at the end with the file a little, and then it held,

and Fred could plainly hear it act upon the lock.

The door was open.

"This is capital" said Fred.

"Hush!" said Jacks, "if you have any regard for our safety, and blow out the light. There is a watchman in the yard."

"The devil there is!" said Fred, in a whisper, as he at once extinguished the light.

"Stand, where you are a little, while I ascertain at what part of his round he is."

They both stood up against the door, which was painted of a dark color, and there, in the most profound stillness, they waited for the watchman to come round, and in the course of a few minutes they heard his footsteps, and his monotonous cry of—

"All's right.—All's right."

The cry was forced every now and then to be uttered by the watch in the wards of Newgate, and in such a tone, too, that it might be audible from yard to yard, so that those who were upon the night-duty could reply to each other.

The watch had a lantern, but he let it dangle at his waist, and walked on without taking any particular notice, as it was his duty undoubtedly to do, of the doors and windows upon his beat.

"We are safe," whispered Jacks. "He has gone by."

Now we must try to get over the wall; and yet there is a door, which, if we could only force, would lead us into the chapel, and from the roof of that we could all but step on to a portion of the

wall. and so let ourselves down in a very
obscure part of Newgate Market.

"That would be much the best plan.
Mr. Jacks, if it could but be carried out."

"Come on then. We must be quick
about it, or we shall have the watch on
his round again."

Fearless Fred was but too willing, and
he followed the housebreaker with alac-
rity.

From the way in which Jacks moved,
it was quite evident that he was well
acquainted with the interior of Newgate,
a knowledge which could only have been
obtained by a frequent incarceration
within its walls.

They soon reached a rather obscure
corner of the prison wall.

"Is it fast?"

"Yes. No, by heaven! it is not,
except upon this side. I have it open
already!"

"And will it lead us to liberty?"

"I hope so. It conducts to the chapel,
as I told you, and from the gallery of
that building there will be no difficulty
in getting on to the roof, and from the
roof there will be no difficulty in getting
to the bit of outer wall that I spoke to
you of, and so letting ourselves carefully
down into the obscure court by Newgate
Market. Keep close to me. I almost
think now that we may consider we have
escaped. But have you any arms?"

"None."

"Take this knife, then. If the worst
should come to the worst, and we happen to encounter any one, it will serve
to defend you. I feel as if I could fight
a hundred men rather than be dragged
back to that abominable cell, which has
all but driven me mad during the time
I have been in it."

Fred took the proffered knife in silence; and with immense speed they
made their way towards the chapel,
which Jacks contrived to enter by picking the lock of another door, and they
found themselves in the still solitude of
that portion of Newgate. They took
the precaution to close the door after
them, and to shoot a couple of bolts into their sockets, so that any surprise
would be not so likely to occur to their
discomforture.

CHAPTER X.

CONTAINS SOMETHING MORE ABOUT
THE CEDAR-BOX.

The gallery of the chapel of Newgate
was reached by a winding staircase of
about forty steps, and they soon ascend-
ed them. Then Jacks led the way to a
window, which he very carefully opened.

"Mr. Fred," he said, "a little dexterity
will be required here."

"In what respect?"

"Why, the roof, or rather the part of
it which we want to get on, which is, in
truth, a gutter connected with it, is just
above the window."

"Well, there is not much difficulty."

"No, to a cool head and steady hand
there is none; but you will have to stand
on the window-sill and lay hold of a portion of the gutter, and so raise yourself
up with the aid of your hands only."

"I think I can do that."

"Good. I know I can—that is to say
if I have not been too much enfeebled
by my three months sojourn in the cell.
But I will try it. Now Mr. Fred, take

your choice: will you go first or shall I?"

"As you say you are a little enfeebled or dread that you may be so, I will go first, and when I am above I can lend you a hand; and if once I have a hold of you, you may depend that I shall not let you fall again."

"You are very kind, Mr. Fred, so I will follow you."

Upon this, Fred, without any hesitation, mounted upon the window-sill outside. The least false step would have precipitated him some sixty feet to one of the inner courts of the prison; but he took good care that he would not make a false step.

It was as much as he could do to reach the roof from where he was; but he did contrive to get a good clutch of it, and then he drew himself up by his hands. In struggling with his feet for a foothold, he broke a pane of glass but probably by so doing he saved himself from a fall for it enabled him to place his foot, lightly on the window frame, and in another moment he was on the roof in safety. Jacks soon followed.

"Which way are we to go now?" said Fred. "You had better lead the route."

"I will. Crouch down and follow me."

After crawling the whole length of the gutter, they turned a corner, and then, by the dim night light, Fred saw that the outer wall of a portion of Newgate was just within arms-length of them, and he could not help exclaiming—

"We are safe!"·

"I think we are," said Jacks. "I have got a rope, with the strong hook at the end of it, round my waist."

"That's all right, and if this iron-work at the top of the wall answers no other good purpose, it will help us to bid adieu to Newgate. Ah, you must be careful of it, Jacks."

"How so?"

"A portion of it revolves, I find."

"That is well thought of. We must take care where we fasten our cord, or it is a case of broken neck with us both, as sure as we are here, Fred."

It certainly did require care to fix the rope to a portion of the iron-work that was a fixture; but when they knew what they had to provide against, that was tolerably easily done, and both Fred and Jacks felt satisfied that the rope was as secure as if it had been fixed to St. Paul's.

"Will you go first?" said Fred.

"No, Mr. Fred, you are the lightest weight, I take it, by a good stone and a half, so you go first. The rope is sure to stand you, but if I were to go first and it were to break with me, you would be in a very awkward situation indeed; so you go first, and I will take my chance afterwards."

"That is generous of you, Jacks."

"Not at all. I do all I can for the best for both of us. I want us to get clear away together, and if we can't, I don't wan't to sacrifice you and do myself no good at the same time. If I break my neck, it is better that you should be in Newgate Market than on the roof of this chapel, I rather think."

"Decidedly so."

"Then be off at once. I will steady the rope as well as I can from the top here, and when you get to the bottom, you can steady it for me from below, you know."

"I can and will."

It was rather an awkward thing to scramble over the iron-work on the top of the wall, and in so doing, Fearless Fred tore both his clothes and his skin in several places; but at length he did get clear of it, and got a fair hold of the rope, which was thick and strong, so that he felt no fear about its carrying him in perfect safety.

"You are sure it is long enough, Mr. Jacks."

"Quite—quite. You may rely upon that."

"Then down I go. Good bye."

Fred was as active as a cat in anything in the shape of climbing, so that to let himself down by the rope was to him a matter of not the least difficulty; only when he got to the end of it, he was a little alarmed to find that he did not touch the ground with his feet, and it was too dark for him to see how far he was from it; so it was rather a nervous thing to let go the rope in such a state of uncertainty as to how far he had to drop.

He hesitated for a few minutes, and then made up his mind to risk it, and shutting his eyes, he let go of the rope.

Plump he came upon his back, for he was not above six inches from the ground, after all.

A sickening sensation came over him at the moment of falling, for he knew not but that might be his last moment in this world; but the revulsion of feeling was immense when he did recover from that supposition. He felt as if a new life had been given to him.

"All's right," he whispered to Jacks, but his companion was too far off to hear him, and kept shaking at the rope to ascertain that all was well below, where upon Fred tightened the rope, and said in a much louder voice, so that Jacks could not fail to hear him if he were at all listening—

"Come on, now. All's right—all's right."

Upon this, Mr. Jacks ventured to commence the descent, which so long as the rope held together, and did not come loose from the iron-work at the top of the wall, was a matter attended by no danger whatever.

In half a minute Jacks was safely by the side of Fred, and then he drew a long breath, saying—

"Thank God, that is over."

"It is a good job done I admit," said Fred; "but it was no very difficult enterprise, after all. Where shall we go to now?"

I wish, Mr. Fred, you would decide that question, but at all events, let us get as far from this neighborhood as we can before daylight."

"Yes, that is the first thing to do. Come on."

They went at a quick pace through a portion of Newgate Market, which was then a much more miserable place than it is now, and had some nooks and corners in it that were truly dreadful, and the haunts of the most outrageous vice.

They were quickly in Newgate Street, however, and then taking their route down Snow Hill, they almost ran up Holborn, although they did not like to make very great speed, for fear of attracting the attention and suspicion of the watch.

As they passed St. Andrew's church,

the clock struck four, and even then a dim light was beginning to creep over the eastern sky.

"We must get out of the town, if we can," said Fred, "before daylight, and I don't know that we can do better than go on up this road."

"Who put you in Newgate?" asked the housebreaker, as they proceeded along.

"Peter Bayley, replied Fred.

"What!" exclaimed Jacks, with an air of surprise, "is he an enemy of yours, too?"

"Yes—a relentless one. But why do you ask? Did he jug you?"

"Aye. I foolishly refused to give him half of my earnings, and he pulled me. I offered him a quarter, aye, even a third; but nothing less than *half* would satisfy him. As I declined according to this exorbitant demand, he had me arrested, and conveyed to his own house, where he kept me seven or eight weeks, in hope of bringing me to terms, but finding my obstinacy equal to his own, he threw me into Newgate."

"He is not one to stop at trifles," observed Fred.

"Not he. And yet, while at his house, I had rare opportunities of studying his character. For all his power, he has his fear-spells as well as other men. For instance, *you* gave him considerable anxiety."

"I?" demanded Fearless Fred, in surprise.

"You. You have or had a cedar box, which is of some importance to him. The loss of it appeared, at times, to drive him almost crazy."

"Indeed! This fellow is not what I took him for!" muttered Fred, to himself. "I must keep an eye on him! And so," he said, aloud, "Peter Bayley was in trouble about the cedar box—eh?"

"Yes, he used to walk up and down his room, muttering and cursing about it in the most extraordinary manner He evidently sets great value upon it, and all I can say is, that if you have got it, you had better take care of it."

"If," said Fred, "I had any box, cedar or otherwise, that I thought Bayley was very anxious about, I should not feel inclined to make it a present to him."

"It's the contents, I rather think, and not the box, that Bayley wants."

"No doubt."

"And so again, I advise you to keep it close."

"If I had it I would," said Fred.

"Then you have it not?"

"If I had, I should hardly feel inclined to say so; but did not Peter say what was in it that made it so valuable to him?"

"Why no—papers only, that was all."

"Oh, well, let him look after his own course, and I will look after mine. All we have to do, Mr. Jacks, is to escape to some place of safety, and then we will bid each other good-bye, and wish each other good fortune."

"So we will," said Jacks, "so we will, Mr. Fred."

From the moment that Jacks had begun to talk about the cedar-box, Fred had been upon his guard. It would not be a fact if we were to say that even before that he had had no suspicions that something amiss was going on, and that Jacks was playing a part; but now there came over his mind a feeling of confirmation of such a fact that he could not any longer resist or do battle with.

As yet, however, all was certainly nothing but suspicion, and that too of the most vague and uncertain character, so that Fred determined to act with great caution in the affair.

One thing however, he quite made up his mind to, and that was by no means to take Mr. Jacks to where Jane was concealed with the cedar-box and Blake.

"Now, Mr. Fred," said Jacks, when they got to the corner of Tottenham Court Road, "this will lead us to the north of London if we pursue that track, and I must throw myself entirely upon you to say if you have any special means of securing our safety in that direction."

"No, Mr. Jacks, I have not."

"Well, then, there is no occasion to go that road. What do you say to going West-end, now?"

Fearless Fred was silent for a few moments, and Jacks, by the early morning light, looked intently in his face, as he said.—

"You seem vexed about something. What is it, Mr. Fred? We are now friends and companions, and it is as well that we share all each other's joys and sorrows."

"Why, Mr. Jacks, I am seriously thinking about the best course for us to pursue for our mutual safety, and I am quite convinced that we had better at once separate."

"Separate?"

"Yes, I feel certain that we had better do so for several reasons, however heart-rending it may be for us to bid adieu to each other."

Jacks would have needed to be a much less acute man than he was, not to catch the ironical character of the tone in which Fred uttered these few words. He made no remark however upon that head, and Fred continued—

"Our escape will soon be found out, Mr. Jacks, and one of the first facts of any importance connected with that discovery will be that we are together."

"True—true!"

"Well then, of course there will be an accurate description of us given to all the police, and we shall be posted in the hue-and-cry at once, as two persons of such a description; but if we separate, we decrease our danger, and by no means draw upon us individually so much observation."

"Well, perhaps so."

"Now, this is a good road up Oxford Street to the west; here is another up Tottenham Court Road to the north. You take one and I will take the other, and you may please yourself which you choose, for it is a matter of the greatest possible indifference to me."

"You don't say so? By-the-by, though, Mr. Fred, now I come to think of it, Peter Bayley, in addition to raving about that cedar-box, used to say something, too, about a young lady that he took it into his head was with you, and whom he wanted to get hold of very much."

"Ah!" said Fred. "Which is your road, west or north?"

"I will go with you, Fred," for I do not quite agree with you in the propriety of parting company so soon. We may be attacked in the streets, and then I shall be able to strike a blow in your defence. If we were further off in the country, I should say part by all means; but now, it would convey to my mind the feeling as if I had deserted you."

"Come on, then."

Fred did not feel inclined in the streets of London to get up a positive quarrel with Mr. Jacks, for he knew that a slight call, provided he was inclined to play the traitor would bring the watch about them; so he made up his mind to temporise with the fellow yet awhile.

With this understanding, they jogged on pretty well together up Tottenham-court-road, and Jacks made no further allusion, either to the cedar-box, or to Jane, for he probably saw that now Fred was thoroughly upon his guard, it would be no use to do so.

The morning came on with rapid strides; and by the time they reached the then village-like suburb of Camden Town, it was quite light enough to see every object with the most perfect distinctness. Then there was a little hesitation as to whether they should go to the right or to the left; but after some time, Jacks inclined to the left, so that they could get through Kentish Town to Highgate.

The countenance of Jacks had a more sinister and strange expression each minute, now, as they went on; and finally they reached Highgate Rise, and entered upon the village.

"I am getting rather tired," said Jacks.

"Never mind that," said Fred. "What is fatigue in comparison to Newgate! On—on, my friend."

"And I am hungry decidedly, and thirsty."

"Never mind hunger and thirst," said Fred. "Come on, and think of Newgate."

Fred was well-pleased to find that Jacks was getting rather tired of trudging on so many miles, and he thought that if he could tire him out that way it would do capitally.

"I am determined to get as far away as possible," added Fred. "Finchley is right along this way."

"Finchley! But you don't mean to walk all that distance?"

"Yes, I do; and beyond Finchley we shall come to Barnet, which is a very nice old town; and there is Hadley then; and then by walking on we shall come to——"

"Oh, stop, stop. You don't suppose I am a machine, do you, that can go on, on, on, without resting?"

"But I am not tired."

"Very likely; you are younger than I am by a considerable deal, and that makes a difference. Here we have walked at a good pace some six miles already, and I tell you that I am not used to this sort of thing, and cannot keep it up much longer."

"Well, Mr. Jacks, it comes just to this, then—I can, and will walk on for the next twenty miles."

"Twenty!"

"Twenty. I know my own powers, and what I can do, and what I can't; and so I advise you to come on with me as long as you can, and when you feel certain that you cannot conveniently come any further, it will be then time for us to say good-bye to each other, and part."

"The devil it will! I have hardly a

leg to stand on now. Where are we at this moment?"

"Just through Highgate, and yonder is Finchley."

Fred stopped and listened.

"What is that I hear upon the road behind us?" he said. "Is it a horse?"

"Hardly—and yet why not? This is a populous enough road, and there may well be a horse upon it, and no harm to us."

The clatter of a horse's feet at a trot, but not a very sharp one, came plainly enough upon their ears, and presently a mounted man passed them, without taking the smallest notice of them. This man was dressed like a clergyman, and had very gray hair, almost white, which floated rather thickly from under his broad-brimmed hat.— The horse he rode was a first-rate one.

"There, you see," said Jacks, "he is no enemy of ours."

"I see he is not. Come on, Jacks."

Jacks looked at Fred for a moment or two, and then gathering all his strength and perseverance to his aid, he said—

"Well, I will go on till I drop. Come on."

Fred had certainly been in the hope that he should get rid of Mr. Jacks now, for the company of that gentleman became each moment more and more objectionable to him and suspicious. Indeed, the feelings of Fred towards Jacks had got a good way past mere suspicion. He might truly say, that now he knew that Jacks was no better than he should be, indeed, it would have been an excellent thing if Jacks had only been half as good as he should have been.

How to get rid of a man, though, who certainly had helped him out of Newgate, and without whose assistance he could not have possibly escaped—for by the trouble that there was even with Mr. Jack's help. Fred could estimate what it would have been without him—was a very difficult proposition indeed.

The determination with which Jacks walked on now, keeping tolerable pace with Fearless Fred, was truly ludicrous. That he was terribly tired, there could be no doubt in the world, but that he fully meant to keep up as long as he possibly could, there could be likewise no doubt, and Fred now began to ask himself how far he really ought to think of taking his companion without bringing affairs between them to something like a crisis. There was another subject, too, that required Fred to think about, and that was, considering that Jacks was an enemy, and had been set to do all that he had done by no less a personage than Bayley himself, for the express purpose of getting into his, Fred's, confidence, and worming out of his simplicity his important secrets, in what way was it intended to dispose of him, Fred, after that object should be attained?—for, although by the determination of Fred, it would not be attained, yet there could be no doubt that some regular course of action had been laid down for Jacks.

Of one thing only, Fred felt pretty sure, and that was, that Jacks would not attack him personally. Fatigued as he was, and if he had not been, the struggle being one of a doubtful character, it was quite out of the question to suppose for a moment that Jacks would risk it.

So far, then, Fred felt a degree of

safety that made him capable of enjoying the evident discomfiture and fatigue of his companion as they together trudged along the road.

A silence of some five miles' distance had now ensued, and it was broken by Jacks, who said, in a low, persuasive kind of tone—

"Ah, Mr. Fred, what would not Peter give to nab us both now?"

"A good round sum, no doubt," replied Fred.

"Ah, in truth, that he would. By-the-by, though, Mr. Fred, I was very much surprised to find that Bayley was so dreadfully superstitious as he really appears to be."

"Is he so?"

"Oh, yes, to an excess. He will have it that he has seen the ghost of one, Lol—Lol—dear me, I forget the name."

"Indeed," said Fred; "perhaps its Lollypop?"

"Oh, no—no. It wasn't that. But, come, you are only joking. I recollect —it was Lolanti—yes, Lolanti was the fellow's name. Well, he would have it that he saw his ghost, and what makes me think of it and mention it now, was, that some of Bayley's men would have it that it was no such thing, but that you had played Peter some trick. Ha? ha!"

"Ha! ha!" laughed Fred.

"What, you did, then?"

"I? Why, what could possibly put that into your head, Mr. Jacks?"

"You laughed, and so I thought that you meant that to signify that you had played old Peter a trick, that was what made me think so."

"I only laughed, Mr. Jacks, because you did. I saw no joke, but out of courtesy to you I laughed. You can admire my motive, I hope, even at the expense of my sincerity; but I won't laugh again, if you would rather that I should not."

Jacks bit his lip with vexation. There was no making anything of Fred, and as that truth gathered strength each moment in his mind, he began more and more to flag in the walking business.

"For Heaven's sake, Mr. Fred, not so fast," he said. "I can walk, but not at the rate you seem to be inclined to go at."

"I beg your pardon, Jacks, but if I go slow I shall tire myself. It is a peculiarity with me that the further I walk the faster I walk; and I tell you again, that I should think it an evil thing to take you an inch beyond your powers. There is a place called Huddesdon, in Hertfordshire, that I think of going to."

Jacks came to a dead stop.

"The devil you do!"

"Yes, and as we shall take that road which is to the left of here, I don't know but what, after all, it will be the wisest thing we can do to push on to St. Albans. It is not very far, and there, as it is a tolerably populous place, we can escape every observation, I dare say, for a time. But who comes here?"

"Why, as I'm a sinner," said Jacks, "it's the same clergyman who passed us upon the road before. You may depend, Fred, that he has been to pay a visit, and is now on his return. What a nice looking old gentleman he is, to be sure. Is he not?"

"Oh, very; quite fatherly," said Fred.

The clergyman trotted on with the utmost gravity, and when he got close to Fred and Mr. Jacks, he said, in a voice of great suavity—

"Can you tell me the time of day ?"

"No," said Jacks suddenly, before Fred could open his watch to reply, "I am sorry, sir, that we don't know the time of day yet."

"Thank you all the same," said the clergyman.

With quite a benign smile, such as some fat pluralist might use upon being inducted to another living that he never intended to attend to, except so far as to pocket the income, the clergyman rode on.

To Fred's apprehension, there was a significance about the question and answer between the clergyman and Jacks that set all his thoughts in a whirl ; and at last he came to the conclusion that the road was watched, and that, in point of fact, he was only let go a little way, something after the fashion that a cat lets go a mouse, merely for the pleasure of making a dash at it again, and enjoying the gratification of a fresh capture. Of course, the object was to get from Fred the particulars of the affairs concerning which Peter Bayley was in such an agony of suspense and apprehension, and then he would be apprehended again, and taken back to Newgate.

A more cunning device than all this, upon the part of Bayley for the purpose of accomplishing his object, without at the same time spoiling his revenge, could not very well have been conceived, for, after all, nothing was more likely than that he, Fred, with the frank suavity of his nature, would tell Jacks everything after they had fairly got away.

As it was, Jacks must have played his part badly in some particular, for Fred was not at all taken in the matter ; and now he had but one thought, and that was, how to get rid of the rascal who was by his side, without at the same time bringing upon himself the attack of those who might be his confederates.

After a little time, they came to a little collection of cottages, and then Fred, as they passed them, spoke in a kindly tone, for he felt himself quite justified in using fraud against fraud.

"Jacks, my good fellow," he said, "you are rather curious."

"Oh, dear, no !"

"But you are, I know, and you think it unkind of me that I do not gratify you upon several points, which I will now clear up satisfactorily."

"Will you ?" said Jacks, eagerly, as he turned right round and took a glance in the direction that the clergyman had gone.

"Yes," added Fred, taking no notice of the movement, although it quite confirmed him, if any confirmation was at all wanted, in his suspicions of the good faith of his traveling companion. "Yes, I will tell you all. If I mistake not, Peter Bayley is very anxious about no less than four things ?"

"Four things ? Four, did you say ?"

"Yes. First of a young lady, named Jane—second, a cedar-box in which there are some rather important papers —thirdly, Blake, his man—fourthly, the ghost, real or supposed, of Lolanti."

"Ah !" said Jacks, and his eye betrayed the eagerness with which he listened.

"Now, Jacks, you must not let what

I am going to say to you go any further, you know, for I would not for worlds have it repeated."

"Oh, no, no, not for the universe!"

How very eager Jacks was! He almost forgot his fatigue and his blistered feet in his agony to hear the statement that he now fully expected was coming from the simple lips of Fred.

With an aspect of great seriousness and mystery, Fred now spoke :—

"You must know, Jacks, that upon Hampstead Heath, if when you turn to the right, after placing your face to the west, and then take two short turnings to the left, and after that go straight on, and keep your right hand to the furze bushes, and your left to a pond, and go as straight as you can for half a mile, you——"

"Stop! stop!"

"No, I can't stop—you come to a well."

"Yes; but, Mr. Fred, upon my life, now, I really cannot follow you. You turn to the right and then turn to the left, and keep the furze bushes to the right, and follow your ——"

Nose."

"Well, well?"

"That was just what I said,—you come to a well,—Confound that clergyman! Here he is again. Of all the restless dignitaries of the church that ever I saw, he beats them. Where can he be going to, now? He has some one with him, too."

"It is his groom," said Jacks, as the clergyman rode up, with a very grave and sturdy-looking servant in top-boots, and a snuff-colored coat, behind him; and a wonderfully white cravat, too, the servant had, as well as the master. The horse that the groom rode on, was no way inferior to that of the clergyman's himself.

As the latter passed Fred and Jacks, he said, with the same smile that he had used before—

"I regret that I troubled you about the time, but do you happen to have heard any clock? I unfortunately left my watch at home."

"No, no," said Jacks, hurriedly. "No sir, we don't know the time of day, but we soon shall."

"Oh, very good. Pardon me for thus troubling you. Good-day."

The suspicious clergyman and his groom rode on.

"Curse him!" said Jacks.

"Why, Jacks," laughed Fred, "what a passion you are in, to be sure! What has the poor parson done that you should curse him!"

"Nothing—that is, confound—no, no —I mean nothing. I only wish he had been at the bottom of the sea. Do you know, I can't bear to be bothered by a clergyman, Mr. Fred? But as you were saying about this well on Hampstead Heath. A well is easily found. They are not so plentiful as blackberries hardly."

"It's no matter whether it is easily found or not, Jacks. You don't want to find it, I'm sure."

"Oh, no, no. Why should I? Well, go on. I am listening."

"So am I," said Fred. "That clergyman and his groom go at a good pace, don't they? Hilloa! who is this?"

A countryman, with a double-barrelled fowling-piece in his hand, got over a hedge close by.

"Oh, bother him!" said Jacks. "Go on with your story, Mr. Fred. Never mind him. He is nothing to us. Let us walk quicker. I am not nearly so tired now as I was, do you know, and that is strange."

"Very. But stop a bit! I have an idea. Hilloa! hilloa! hoi! there! You fellow with the gun. Hilloa!"

"Goodness gracious!" said Jacks, "what do you want with him?"

"Well, what now?" said the countryman, as he came lazily forward.

"My good fellow," said Fred, "is that your own gun?"

"Why, yes, it ought to be, seeing as I gave a matter of three pound ten for it in London only last year."

"Very well; then, I will give you five guineas for it here upon the spot."

"No, no; you are mad," said Jacks.

"Not so mad as you suppose," said Fred. "Will you take the money, my good fellow, or will you not?"

"Oh, you are a joking, sir, with I," said the countryman. "It's a roughish sort of a gun, although a nice good 'un to go; but it ain't the sort of gun for a gentleman. You are only joking, sir."

"Not I. Here's the money. All I wish is the gun."

"As he spoke, Fred produced the five guineas, and held them out in the palm of his hand to the countryman, who looked eagerly at the coin and then at Fred, and then at the gun. At last he made a grab at the money, as if he thought that if he were not quick about it, Fred would repent of the offer, and return the glittering coin to his pocket again. But as Fred let him take them, he was reassured, and handing him the gun, he said—

"Take it, sir, and may it do you good service—take it, sir, and thank you kindly. It ain't much use to me; for though I do only go out to shoot a rabbit now an' then, it isn't a good thing for a poor man to have a gun when there are preserves all round him. It makes the gentry suspect him like, you see, sir.

"No doubt; and, besides,"—Fred laughed—"besides, you can buy another, you know, and pocket the difference."

"He—he!" laughed the countryman "I can—cood, I can do that, surely, sir. Many thanks to you."

"Stop a bit. Is it loaded?"

"Why, yes. The right-hand barrel with goodish sized shot, and the left-hand with a bullet."

"Good; but you have a flask and powder?"

"Take 'em—take 'em. I had 'em with the gun, and so ought you. Now you are all right, sir; and dang it, I don't feel a bit displeased about my morning's work. Good luck go with you, sir, and the old gun, too, not that it's so old either; good day, sir."

"Thank you—good day."

The countryman walked off, and Fred, by a rapid inspection of the gun, found that it was duly primed, and in good order for use.

"Gracious providence!" said Jacks, and he seemed ready to tear the hair out of his head from vexation, "what do you want with that? You must be mad, quite outright! Why the possession of such a weapon as that will draw down upon us the attention of every one whom we may meet."

" But consider, in the right-hand barrel a lot of goodish sized shot——"

"I tell you, Mr. Fred, that——"

" And in the left a bullet."

" Curse the bullet, and curse the shot !"

" Stop !"

" What for—what for—eh ?"

" My dear Jacks, this seems a very lonely bit of road. We are past all the houses, and I don't see a human being about but ourselves. The clergyman and his groom have ridden on ; and now, my dear Jacks,"—Fred stepped back three or four paces nimbly—" and now, my dear Jacks, as sure as there is a heaven above us, and as that I am a living man, if you don't be off before I can count twenty out of the range of this gun, I'll first give you the goodish sized shot, and then, by Jove, I'll give you the bullet."

Fred presented the gun directly at Mr. Jacks' face, and they contemplated each other for a minute or two in silence. Jacks face looked the color of rather indifferent putty.

" Run !" cried Fred, " or by Heaven you are a dead man !"

" Murder !" shouted Jacks.

" Run, I say or nothing can save you !"

" No—no. Mr. Fred. Stop ! Oh, don't I I will tell you all. Peter Bayley, you see——"

" I know all. Run, you infernal scoundrel, or the shot will be about your ears before you know where you are."

Off set Jacks notwithstanding all his fatigue and the blisters on his toes, at such a rate, that it was quite ludicrous to see him. Once he fell down, but he hardly stopped to gather himself up again, but went along upon all fours, till, quite

as if by accident, he got upon his feet again, and resumed his headlong speed. There was a turn in the road, and Mr. Jacks was out of sight in a moment. Fearless Fred looked up at the sun, and then he glanced at the shadows of the trees in the hedgerows.

" This is my way," he said, and in another moment he was over the hedge and in the meadows on the opposite side. He had hardly got there when he heard the gallop of horses' feet, and he at once flung himself down close under the hedge, but not so low as to prevent him from peeping into the road-way and seeing who it was that were coming.

" Jacks' clergyman, by all that's good," said Fred, as he saw the very sober and pious individual gallop up with his groom. They both passed close to the hedge, and the clergyman, in a loud voice, said—

" I tell you what, Johnstone, that I will blow his brains out the next time I pass them, if Jacks has not succeeded. The fellow is upon his guard, confound him, and the whole affair is a failure."

" I'm afraid it is Mr. Bayley," said the groom.

Fred was astounded. Much as he had heard of Peter Bayley's tact and skill in disguises, he had no idea that he really possessed such a consummate art as to prevent him, Fred, from having the least suspicion of him when attired as a clergyman, and with a false color upon his face, and a wig and painted eyes, all to make him up as an old man. To be sure, the voice in which he had spoken to the seeming groom was the voice of Bayley, and had for the moment staggered Fred ; but yet he could hardly believe it could possibly be him until he heard him named by his man.

After that fact, though, there could be that no doubt but the seeming clergyman was no other than Peter Bayley himself, and that he had been upon the track of Fred and Mr. Jacks from the first step that they took out of Newgate, and that Jacks was pretty well aware of that rather important fact. If Fred, in the sincerity and frankness of his disposition, had spoken freely to Jacks, he would upon one of the occasions of Peter passing them, have found out, to use their own private signal, "what the time of day was," and then Fred would, upon the moment, either have been pounced upon and re-captured, or possibly, if Bayley thought that such a course would answer his purpose best, would have been killed upon the spot, so that he owed entirely his preservation to the fact of keeping his secrets to himself.

From his rather thorny but still sufficiently secure retreat, because it was entirely unsuspected, Fred was able now to hear every word that Bayley said to the man who was with him.

"They ought to be not far off now, Johnstone," he added. "Confound that Jacks, he has not managed matters properly, or he would have had no sort of difficulty in the transaction."

"I don't know, Mr. Bayley," said Johnstone. "If Fred got to suspect him by any means, it would be no easy matter to get at the information you wanted, sir."

"Well, I am out of patience."

"It will be better to give Jacks a little more time, sir, won't it?"

"I don't know that. We will ride on slowly, and meet them again, and hear what Jacks has to say."

Now, from where he was, nothing could have been easier for Fred than to have at once accommodated Peter Bayley with either of the barrels of the charged gun. He could have given him the shot, or he could have given him the bullet that was in the left-hand barrel, and Bayley's career in either case would, in all human likelihood, have come to an end, much to the benefit of society at large, and of him, Fearless Fred, in particular. Little did Peter know his danger.

Once Fred did slowly raise the gun to his shoulder, and cover Bayley with it. One touch to either of the triggers, and the business would have been done; but Fred could not give that touch.

"No, no," he said to himself, "no. It is too much like assassination. I cannot do it—I wish I could, but I cannot. I have no compunction about killing such a man as Bayley, but it must be in fair fight, and not from behind a hedge. I cannot do it."

He lowered the gun again, and Peter Bayley was saved.

"Come on, Johnstone," he said. "Come on at a walk. We won't overtake them soon."

Another moment and they were gone, and then, if Fred had felt ever so much inclined to shoot the villain, it is doubtful if he could have done so. It would have been a long and a very hazardous shot now.

"It is done," said Fred as he rose and looked over the hedge after them. "It is done now and I have let go the greatest villain the world ever saw. Not so would he have allowed me to escape. Oh, no, no! But that is no matter; I am not, and surely I don't want to be, like Peter Bayley.

This was true enough, and Fred with the gun upon his arm, proceeded across the meadow in which he found himself. That he was trespassing upon some one's grounds, who doubtless would be in a great passion if he saw him, there is little doubt; but that did not give much concern to one of so adventurous a cast as Fearless Fred, and he scarcely troubled himself to look to the right or to the left to see if any one were at hand.

Fred in his progress now to where he had left Jane and Blake, was only guided by the sun; that enabled him, at all events, to see that he was going in the right direction; but in crossing the country in the manner that he was, he could not take upon himself to say how far he had to go, or if he was to the right or to the left of the road he wanted to reach.

"Hilloa!" cried a voice near him.

"What now?" said Fred.

"Come, I say," said a countryman, making his way, almost breathless, to where Fred was composedly pursuing his way, "you mustn't come over here, I tell you."

"Oh, very well. I shall know that another time."

"But you must go back."

"Must I! What is on the other side of yonder hedge?"

"Why, the road, to be sure."

"Then I will go to it, my friend, which will be all that you can desire, I presume?"

"No, it ain't. My master says as I am to turn people back, and not let 'em go on at all; so, back you must go."

"Did your master tell you how to make people go back if they would not? I warn you, my fine fellow, to keep your distance, or I shall be obliged to give you the contents of one of the barrels."

The fellow looked aghast.

"Now, look you," added Fred, "I know I am tresspassing now, because you have told me; but all you can do is to warn me off the land, and as I will tell you who I am, that will give the only legal remedy you can have in the matter."

"Who are you, then?"

"The Marquis of Alecumpaine."

"Oh, Lord! I beg your marquis's lordship's pardon, that I does. I am quite sure, that master and missus would be as pleased as possible if your marquis of a lordship's grace would only stop at Toothems."

"At what?"

"Toothems, your worship. That's the name of the place here. Master was a pawnbroker in Bishopsgate, you see, your grace of a marquis; and when he made his fortune and bought this here estate, it was called The Grange, but he altered the name to Toothems, which was missus's maiden name."

Fred laughed. "That will do," he said. "Some other time I will do myself the pleasure of calling. You can give the marquis's compliments to the family, and say that I am very sorry I trespassed upon their land."

"Oh, but my lord marquis, there's five Miss Squapps."

"Miss what do you call them?"

"Squapp is their names, my lord mar

quis, and they want to know a lord ; and if you will only come up to the lodge, how glad they will be. They won't ever forgive me for letting your lordship's grace go."

"And yet go I must. Farewell! Tell them I will call some other time."

Fred reached the hedge, and clambered over it in a moment, and sprung into the road. One glance at that road told him that he was very much nearer to the place where he had left Jane than he had anticipated, and he quickened his pace, until he saw a country lad sitting by the road side, apparently crying. A little bundle and a stick were lying upon the grass by his side, and a broad-brimmed felt-hat concealed his head and the upper part of his face, while the lower was resting upon his hands.

Fred could hear the boy sobbing, and he was wondering what could induce so much grief in one so young as he approached him. The sobs of the boy evidently prevented him from hearing the approach of Fred, and the latter was close enough to him to reach out his hand and place it upon his shoulders, as he said in a kindly tone—

"My poor boy, what is it that fills you so full of grief? Can I aid you in any way, my good fellow?"

"Fred!" shrieked the boy, as he withdrew his hands from before him. "Oh, God! My Fred! My own Fred!"

Fred dropped the gun, and in another moment, Jane, for it was, indeed, no other, fainted in his arms!

The shock of delight—the surprise that for a moment or two bewildered his brain, were almost too much for poor Fred ; and he, too, felt as if a veil had covered the face of nature, and for a time he was scarcely conscious. That feeling rapidly passed away, though, and as he held her whom he loved better than all the world in his arms, and repeatedly kissed her pale cheeks, the tears gushed from his eyes, and he could only faintly say—

"My Jane—my own, dear girl! Oh, speak—speak to me!"

With a faint sigh she opened her eyes, and looked at him. Her little hands clutched him tightly by his dress.

"Oh, no—no," she said, "you must not go from me! It is not a dream! Oh, no, do not tell me it is all a dream, and that you are going to leave me!"

"I will not—I am not."

"Fred—Fred! You are my Fred, and I have you with me now. Oh, God! let him stay—let him stay with me!"

The overcharged heart of the young girl now found relief in tears ; and she wept for some few moments upon Fred's breast. They were blessed, peace-giving tears, those; and Fred did not try to check them. He knew, little as his experience was, that those tears would bring relief to Jane.

After a time, then, she was able to look up to him again, and to smile in his face, as she said—

"Ah! now, dear Fred, I know that you are with me, and that it is all real, this happy meeting. You came to me, Fred——".

"By accident, dear Jane—only by accident, just now ; but I was coming to you. What a joy it is to have met you.

"Yes, Fred—yes! Newgate!—Ah! that dreadful name! You were there, in the dismal prison. Have they let you go free?"

"No. I am free, but with no good will of those who would have kept me a prisoner. But I am all amazement to find you here, and alone."

"I will tell you how that is. You shall know all that, Fred. Oh, let me look at you first. You are pale, my Fred."

How she clung to him, and with what a world of rapturous fondness she looked up in his face!

"What do you start at, Fred?" she added. "You look along the road, too, as though you had some fears."

"I have fears, Jane. This is too public a road for me to remain on long. Bayley, my worst enemy, and the worst enemy that any mortal man could have, is in this immediate neighborhood."

"Peter Bayley?"

"Yes. Let us get to some more retired spot than this, Jane; and then you shall tell me what has happened to you since we last met. I think I see the opening of a shadowy lane a little further on yonder, by the old chestnut tree."

The shady lane that had been mentioned was soon reached, and they went some little distance along it. The trees quite met overhead in that lane, making a natural and beautiful verdant arch, through small crevices in which the daylight peeped most deliciously. It was evidently a very little frequented spot; although the marks of carriage wheels showed that it led to somewhere or another.

"Now, my Jane," said Fred, "tell me how it is, that I see you alone, and thus attired?"

"Oh, this is the Sunday suit of a lad that came to the cottage. But, Fred, I want to know how you got out of prison."

"Yes; but——"

"Nay, Fred, you must tell me your adventures first. Do, dear Fred."

"Well, I will. Only you know, that I am so much more interested in you, than you can possibly be in me, that——"

"Fred!"

"Well, my darling Jane! What is it?"

"How can you be so wicked and so unkind as to speak to me in that way! Ah, you are smiling! You know what an injustice you did me. Fred—Fred, it is very cruel of you—very cruel, indeed."

"I will tell you all about it in a few words," said Fred; and he related what is already known to the reader.

Jane sighed, as he concluded.

"Ah! Fred," she murmured, "you must live to be something different—something better than you are now. You are yet young, Fred, and surely you will not waste a whole life in such perils as those which now surround you?"

"Do not speak to me of that now, Jane; but tell me as nearly as you can where the cedar-box is?"

Jane gave Fred now such an accurate description of the place in which she had hidden the cedar-box, that he could not possibly miss it; and then she told him that the reason she was alone when he met her was, that the cottage where she had been staying was attacked by four men, who had offered a hundred pounds to the lad, Philip, to bring her out to them; but that, on the contrary, he had brought her the dress she then wore, and urged her to fly. What had become of Blake, she had no sort of idea.

"Jane," said Fred, "you are still, no doubt, hunted far by your implacable enemies, the earl and his wife; but, please Heaven, I will yet protect you from them. I must place you somewhere in safety in London, and then go and get the cedar-box, which, I am convinced, contains papers that will unravel the mystery attaching to your birth and name. You may be some great person, Jane."

"Never so great, and never so happy," said the young creature, as she fell upon Fred's breast, as when I'm with you, dear Fred, and know that you love me."

"Hush! What do you hear now?"

"Horses feet."

"So do I. This won't do. Peter Bayley is about this part of the country. He will be furious at my escape."

At this moment, a creaking of branches, fell upon their ears. Fred, seizing his gun, started up, and beheld five men breaking through the bushes, and almost upon him. In their leader, he recognized one whom he knew but too well.

"Peter Bayley!" he exclaimed.

"Aye, Peter Bayley!" was the reply of that personage, with a roar of triumph. "Upon him, men!" he added, turning to his companions. "Arrest him—dead or alive, I care not. Should he resist, kill him!"

"Caught at last!" muttered Fearless Fred. "But I'll die game, come what may of it!"

He raised the gun to his shoulder, and, quick as light, pulled the trigger.

"Devil!" he exclaimed, "if I must die, it shall be for ridding the earth of a monster! Take that!"

A roar of agony broke from the lips of Peter Bayley, who, in another moment, fell, like a lifeless ox, outstretched upon the earth.

A volley of pistol shots followed, and Fearless Fred fell. It appeared to him as though he were shot through the head; but yet by some means he managed to get to his feet, and by an impulse rather than from any reflection, he ran forward, and stumbled over some shrubs and fell again. There was a splashing of water beneath him, and he faintly struggled for a moment or two. He heard a shrieking voice cry "Fred! Fred!" and then the world seemed to be twisting round with him, at a mad gallop, and he lapsed into total insensibility.

Death could have been no more to Fearless Fred than that dreadful feeling when he found that sense and thought were alike fading from him.

How long he lay in that trance of death, Fearless Fred had not the least idea. It might have been an hour—a day—a week for all he knew; but he felt suddenly a pain at his head that forced a scream from his lips. As he approached consciousness, he heard, or fancied he heard voices and footsteps, and then a scream, and then a confusion of voices, and some one said—

"It is some one badly hurt. Lend me your pitcher, my little girl."

Splash—splash came cold water in Fred's face, and he felt much revived. He was able to open his eyes, and then he saw bending over him a tall female, with a pair of spectacles on, who was from an earthenware pitcher, dashing water in his face. It was such a relief to Fred to get rid of the faintness, that he murmured faintly—

"Thank you—God bless you!"

"Don't say that," replied the tall female in the spectacles. "It is but a slight service. But how came you in this state? You are but a boy. How is it that you are in such a condition?"

"Such a thief," said Fred, gaspingly. "Oh, such a villain! Thank you, madam. Oh, God, if I could only feel sure that she were safe! I care nothing for myself, but much I think of her."

"Whom speak you of?"

Fred looked at the tall lady, and then shook his head sadly. His heart was too full just then to allow him to utter even the name of Jane, which was upon his lips.

"Come—come," said the lady, "you must not be pestered just now with questions. The first thing is to serve you, and to attend to your wounds. Phebe—Phebe!"

"Yes, mum," said the little girl, who kept at a certain distance.

"You run to my house, and tell James to come here directly."

The little girl ran off, and then Fred just managed to say, as he fixed his eyes wistfully upon the pitcher—

"Water! water!"

"To be sure," said the tall lady with the spectacles. "I ought to have thought of that.

Fred drank from the pitcher as she held it to him, and he felt much relieved as he did so.

"More thanks," he said. "Oh, madam, I don't think I am much hurt, and you have saved me from such a world of pain. I think if that dreadful insensibility had come over me again I should never have seen the light of day more.

"And so young, too. Why, you are not twenty?"

Oh, here is James. Now, James, you will assist this wounded youth to the house."

James took up Fearless Fred in his arms as if he had been some little child, and walked on with him as easily as possible."

"Where will you have him put, missus?"

"In the visitors' room, James," said the tall lady; "and here, Phebe, where are you?"

"Here, madam," said Phebe.

"Go to Mr. Moore, the surgeon, in the village, and tell him, with my compliments, that I would be glad to see him as soon as he can come to my house."

"Yes, ma'am."

The little girl started off in a moment, while Fred was carried to the house of the tall lady in the spectacles.

We may as well now state that that lady's name was Block, and that she was in independent circumstances. The house, old-fashioned as it was, belonged to her, and she was, with the little that she possessed, perfectly rich, because it was enough for her simple desires, besides leaving her a surplus, which it was her delight to make use of in works of kindness and charity.

Fred was so much refreshed by the draught of water that he had had from the earthen pitcher, that he could very well now have walked to the house, but James would not let him, but carried him all the way.

The visitors' room at Rose Cottage, for that was the name of the pleasant little abode of Mrs. Block, was one of the prettiest chambers in the whole place. The window was quite overrun with honeysuckle and roses, and the sweet-scented clematis, and the room itself was quite a little *bijou* in the way of decorations and furnishing.

In one corner was the bed, with its pink and lace hangings; and if that bed had been taken out of the room you would have taken the place to be a very pretty country boudoir, or sitting-room—for there was nothing cheap or flaring about the place, just on account of its being a bed-room—and nothing else.

Poor Fred, though, had not much time nor inclination upon his first introduction to that apartment to look at it or its decorations. The pain at the side of his head was very great. That pain was external, though, and that made it endurable, for it did not attack his brain in any way; therefore, he had all his presence of mind to bring to bear upon it, and to support him under it, which would not have been the case had the smarting been internal instead of external, so that upon the whole Fred did not much mind it. He began, however, to find out various other little hurts, and one of his shoulders felt

very stiff and tender.

Here you are!" said James, as he placed Fred on the sofa in the room "How do you feel now!"

"Better, decidedly."

"Well, I'm glad of that, and now you had better get off some of them things of yours, that are all wet, you see; but I'll be hanged if I know what you are to put on besides."

"Nor I, either. I had better get to bed, I suppose, and yet, no. Now that I come to look about me, it would, I see, be a thousand pities for me, with my torn and draggled apparel, and all this blood upon me, to make no end of mess in this pretty room. I will go down stairs, James. I daresay you have some back kitchen, or, perhaps, a yard with a pump, and if so, I will soon put myself to rights."

"No," said a voice, and Mrs. Block made her appearance. "No, I will not have you do so. James, never mind about the room, but assist this guest of mine to change his apparel."

"But, ma'am, what has he to put on!"

Mrs. Block was rather posed at this, and she reflected for a little while, and then she said—

"It is true that we have no male clothing in the house excepting yours, James, and they would be a world too large for my young friend here. Go to yonder press, and—Yet no, I will go myself. You must not touch what is there. Poor Maria's clothes are there, and she was about the size of this poor lad. By-the-by, what is your name, my young friend!"

"Fred, madam."

"That is your christian name ?"

"It is, madam ?"

Mrs. Block was quick-sighted enough when she had her spectacles on, so that she saw that Fred did not wish to state his other name before James, at all events, and she would not press the question then, but took from the press that was in the room a black silk dress, and handing it to Fred, she said—

You can put that on for the present, till James has dried your clothes by the kitchen fire. I will come to you soon, and I beg that you will consider this house as your home for the present."

"You are too kind to me, madam."

"No, I am only doing what it pleases me to do. It is my duty, that is all."

Mrs. Block now left the room, and by the assistance of James, Fred got rid of his wet garments, and then, just as he was preparing to replace them by the black silk dress that his kind protectress had lent to him, there was a tap at the door, and immediately an elderly gentleman appeared upon the threshold.

"That is Doctor Moore," said James.

"Well, James, what is all this about ?" said the doctor. "Your mistress tells me that there is a young gentleman here, who has been beset by thieves. I hope it is nothing serious ?"

"Not at all, sir," said Fred, "I assure you."

"That's right. Where is the hurt ?"

"This side of my head, sir. I think, with the exception of a few bruises, I am all right everywhere else ; but my head does, indeed, pain me."

The doctor was a man of skill, and he rapidly removed the coagulated blood from the wound at the side of Fred's head, and then he said—

"This has been a close touch. I can trace the path of a bullet right along the head. It has torn up the scalp in its path, and slightly bruised the bone.—Why, my young friend, if that bullet had been but the eighth of an inch to one side, it would have taken off the curve of your temple, and killed you at once."

"A good shot, sir," said Fred.

"Too good by a great deal. I suppose it stunned you ?"

"Yes, sir ; I rather think that I fell into a ditch, and lay there for some hours, till I was found by Mrs. Block. There is no necessity for laying up, is there ?"

"Yes, for a day or two. Then, if nothing happens wrong or awkward with the wound, you will be all right again."

"Thank Heaven !"

The doctor paid no attention to the ejaculation upon the part of Fearless Fred, nor did he ask any further questions upon the subject of the wound at all, but contented himself by doing his professional duty, and he left Fred much relieved by the proper dressing that his wound had. When he was gone, Fred got on the black silk dress, and it was quite astonishing how well it fitted his slim and youthful figure, so that James was quite astonished, and could not help saying to him—

"Indeed, sir, if anybody was only to come into the room in a hurry, they might take you for a young lady. But I'll soon dry your clothes, sir, in the kitchen."

"Do so, James, for I assure you I feel anything but comfortable with this kind of apparel on me."

James left Fred to himself; and then, as soon as the door was closed and our hero found himself alone, he flung himself into a chair, and clasping his hands, he said—

"Oh, Jane! Jane! what is your fate? What has become of you, deprived of my protection? My heart is full of agony for you. I must leave this place in search of you as soon as possible, or I shall go mad with apprehension. Suspense will kill me!"

Fred heard a slight rustling as of apparel, and upon looking up, he saw Mrs. Block in the room.

Fred looked confused.

"Well," said Mrs. Block, "the surgeon tells me that, although you have had a narrow escape, your hurts are in reality but trifling; and in the case of a bullet, why, I suppose an inch is as good as a mile, is it not?"

"Yes, madam; yes. How much I have to thank you!"

"Not at all, Fred—I think you told me that your name was Fred, did you not?"

"I did, madam; but I did not tell you my other name. Fred is my christian name. Oh, madam, you have been very kind to me. You have, without inquiring as to whether I was deserving of such kindness, sheltered me in your house. You have taken me in and played the part of the good Samaritan to me, and I feel that to deceive you would be but an ill return for your goodness. I am Fearless Fred, and the world will tell you that my profession is—is—"

"Go on," said the lady, calmly.

"To rob upon the highways," added Fred. "I am Fearless Fred, the highwayman. And now, madam, you know enough to hang me."

"Alas!" said the lady, "can this be possible?"

"It is true—it is too true. I am so distracted at this moment for the fate of one who is dearer to me than all the world beside, that I know not what to say to you, and death would be a release to me from the pains of my mind, were it not that I feel I have a duty still to do towards that woman."

Mrs. Block sat down upon a chair opposite to Fred, and looked at him in silence for some few moments. By the expression of her countenance it was quite clear that she was very much affected.

"This is a great grief to me," she said at length. "I can hardly think it possible that one so young as you are, and one, as it were, yet upon the very threshold of existence, should have given himself up to such a course. Are you telling me the truth?"

"I am, madam."

"Then it is very—very sad."

"You feel that I am not a fit guest for you to harbor here," said Fred, as he rose. "I will leave you at once, madam. I might, merely by a forged tale, have deceived you as to who and what I was; but let my faults and vices and crimes be what they may, no one can accuse me of ingratitude or falsehood.— Were it at the certain peril of my life I could not but have told you the truth; and now I leave you, blessing you, and thanking you for all that you have done for me."

"In that dress?" said Mrs. Block, in a low tone. "Do you mean to go away in that dress?"

Fred was recalled at these words to the consciousness that he had a black silk gown on, and he looked a little confused, as he said—

"I must wait until James brings me my own apparel, I suppose. Then, madam, I will hasten to relieve you from my presence."

"You will do no such thing," said the lady, while a tear stole down her cheeks· "I look upon your being here as a direct interposition of Providence in your behalf, and as a great mercy to me that Heaven has thought fit to make me the means of restoring you to a life of virtue and usefulness. You shall not leave here. I will protect you. All I ask of, you is, that you will tell me, if you can frankly and freely, that you will sin no more."

"Alas! I dare not!"

"You dare not tell me so, or dare not sin? Which am I to think?"

"That I dare not make such a promise to you."

"Well, it is better that you should not, perhaps, for that shows that you doubt your own power. That power, though, when once awakened, will grow into strength; and if I can only save you from the dreadful fate that awaits you, if you continue in your course of crime, this will be a very happy day for me."

"Hear me, madam," said Fred. "I can fully appreciate and understand your goodness, and your wish to do all in your power for me, but there is no such thing in this world for me as another path than that which I have already chosen. The law and the myrmidons of the law will not permit me to retrace my steps. I am already a criminal, and there is nothing before me but the death of one, or that life of daring and peril that may ward off such a fate for a time."

"You are wrong."

Fred shook his head.

"You do not know, madam, so well as I do that when the line is passed that separates right from wrong, there is no retreat."

"There is a retreat. Your full and free pardon from the crown would surely save you, would it not?"

"Oh, yes; but ——"

"I will get it for you. I never asked a favor yet of one who can grant such favors if she pleases, and who more than once has asked me if I had such a boon to ask. The Queen knows me, and will not refuse me."

"The Queen, madam?"

"Yes; she will, for me, ask of the King your free pardon, and with that in your possession, surely all will be well and your own path will be freely open before you."

Fred looked at the lady for a moment, and the tears gushed to his eyes, and holding both his hands upon his face he said—

"Oh, Jane—Jane, where are you? What has become of you, that you cannot hear this? It is a dream, though, only a dream. No, madam, you would be refused. You do not know my career. You see that I look young, and I am what I look; but you cannot guess at the adventures that I have passed through. There is no mercy in this world for me: I am an outcast of society. All men's hands are lifted against me. I am hunted, so you will not wonder that at times I have turned upon the hunters."

"Tell me strictly, if you can, what you have the most to fear. Tell me the minor incidents of your life, and then let me judge of your situation."

"I will—I wil.."

With great rapidity, Fred sketched the history of his life to Mrs. Block. She heard him with marked attention, and then she said, in a low tone—

"Poor Fred! and is that all?"

"It is madam, except little matters of no import."

"Why, my poor boy, your time has been, for the most part spent in the protection of the young girl you speak of."

"Yes, it has; and if I had a hundred lives, I would lay them all down to save her from a single pang."

"But you think you have killed the villain, Bayley?"

"I hope so."

Mrs. Block shook her head at these words.

"Do not say you hope so," she said. "I hope quite the contrary. But wait in peace here. I will make the necessary inquiries for you. For a day or two you should remain here until I am able to bring you positive information. Be assured I have both the means and the will to procure it."

"And can you still, after knowing who and what I am, make me welcome to your house?"

"I can. Your history is a more eventful than criminal one. I will not say that you have not committed crimes, for you have done so; but still, there is nothing that might not, upon the assurance of a different life for the future, be easily forgiven. Rest in peace."

"But, Jane?"

"I doubt not, Fred, but I shall be able to ascertain something concerning her. It is quite impossible that such

events as you have related could take place upon the highway, and no notice taken of them. The news of the attempt to take you, and of the riot in consequence, and of your escape, must be, even by this time, well known. You are perfectly safe here, though, I think and hope; so now be still and calm while I go to get news for you, and be assured that I will return with some as early as possible."

Fred could not find language in which to express his thanks to Mrs. Block. It seemed to him as if a mountain were lifted off his heart, at the idea that she would do all in her power to get him intelligence of Jane. To remove from where he was without some authentic news regarding her, he felt would be madness; so he schooled himself to patience.

"I shall eagerly expect you, madam," he said, "and I will strive to wait in peace till I have the joy of seeing you again."

Mrs. Block left him, and Fred, feeling a sense of great uneasiness, after partaking of a little repast that James had brought him, flung himself upon the sofa and dropped into a profound sleep.

Had our hero known that James, the man-servant was listening at the door of his chamber, and had overhead every word that passed between himself and the benevolent Mrs. Block, he would have considered twice before he laid himself down to sleep.

Let us turn for a few minutes from Fearless Fred, and look after the unhappy Jane.

The body of Peter Bayley was lifted up, by his men, and placed in a carriage, and, together with Jane, conveyed to the thief-taker's house in London. It was many hours after his return ere Peter Bayley recovered from the effects of his wound. When he did, he was quite pale and thoughtful. In fact, his mind was running upon the disastrous results of his attempt to capture Fearless Fred, and how he could wreak his vengeance upon that daring blade. One thing gave him indescribable pleasure, viz: Jane was in

his power. This, in the thief-taker's view, was an important point gained. How, the reader will learn by-and-bye. As soon as he was able to handle a pen, Peter Bayley drew up and despatched the following note :

"Peter Bayley presents his compliments to E. B. and begs to state that *she* is in safe keeping. If E. B. will be so good as to call in Newgate Street,' he may hear all particulars."

In less than an hour after the transmission of this letter, the party to whom it was addressed made his appearance at the thief-taker's, and was shown into the reception room.

On entering the saloon, Peter Bayley beheld a tall, stout man standing by the fire-place.

Our readers have no doubt as to who he is. The earl, who has already to such an extent been the persecutor of Jane was the E. B. to whom Peter Bayley had sent.

"Well, my lord," said Peter, "I'll trouble you to take a good look at me before we proceed to business."

The earl did look at him.

"Dear me, Mr. Bayley, you do not look well. What has happened, pray?"

"I'll tell you, my lord. I have been half killed, and in your service—I have a broken rib and in your service—I am a mass of bruises from top to toe, and all in your service. I don't feel quite sure even that a bullet is not in my head; and if it be, it is all on your account, and in your service. Now, my lord, what do you say to that?"

"I am very sorry."

"Bah! What's the use of sorrow to me? You know that won't heal my wounds, nor compensate me for the pain of them."

"Certainly not," said the earl, as he took out his pocket-book. "Pray accept this one hundred pound note, Mr. Bayley."

"Humph! Well, that is treating one as a gentleman ought, and I will accept it; and so, now, I tell you that I have the girl secure."

"It is the best news that I have heard for some time, Mr. Bayley; and as regards this incubus—this obstruction to all our plans——"

"Your plans, my lord."

"Well—well, my plans, if you will—This Fearless Fred—where is he?"

"That I cannot just now tell you. I have some idea that he is dead, but I can't say for a certainty. If not dead, he is badly hurt, and will either die or fall into my hands soon."

"And—the—cedar-box? have you no news of that to give to me?"

"None. I fear we shall never see it. I feel assured that nothing but accident will ever bring it to light to us. It is in vain to prosecute either Fred or the girl about it. They will be steadfast to their deaths."

The earl was silent for a few moments, and then, with a bitterness that he did not attempt to conceal, he burst out with—

"Oh, that villain, Lolanti! it is he who has brought all this suffering, all this anxiety upon my heart—it was he stole from me the papers, and, afterwards, when he thought to make my purse ever at his command, trusted me with the fact that he had possession of them, and that they were in a cedar box, hidden from me. I could easily have killed him, but of what use would that have been, since the box was hidden? Without it I know not what to do.

"Well, my lord, people I can find—for they must keep above ground to breathe; but a little wooden box may easily be hidden even from me. I can do no more. I say that I have the girl."

"Indeed! Actually beneath this roof—and—and no one knows that you so have her?"

"None but my creatures."

"The countess and I have been thinking about this girl, and we think she has gone through so much that it would be quite as well if she were to die."

"Very likely, my lord."

"What can she have to hope for in this world? No doubt she has been seduced by Fearless Fred, and that's what makes her so fond of him."

"Very likely."

"And so, if for the peace and the credit of everybody she were to die quite suddenly, it would be a good thing; and far—very far, indeed, in my opinion from a fact to be regretted. You understand me?"

"Yes, so far as you've gone."

"A thousand pounds is a large sum, Mr. Bayley."

"It is."

"I tell you, Mr. Bayley, that I would give a thousand pounds to be certain that the girl was dead."

"Say two thousand, and I will do it."

"Agreed."

"Very good; and the countess quite understands this, and agrees with it?"

"She does," said the earl, faintly. "She suggested it!"

"I might have known that, for if anything more desperately cruel than another is suggested against a woman, it is by a woman."

"Peace! Why do you torture me in this way, Bayley. Let it suffice that you earn your money. Do not preach to me the future. I say nothing of the countess. I am nearly mad already."

As for Fearless Fred, I will charge you nothing. I will lump him into the bargain, for I have some private matters to settle with that hasty young gentleman, and I will not rest until I have settled them. As soon as I can sit in the saddle, I will be after him like his fate."

"But, Bayley, do you not think it more than likely he knows all that the papers in the cedar-box could communicate to him?"

"No. If he did, such knowledge would soon show itself by its results. If he knew the story, which it is of such importance that no one but you and I should know, what would hinder him from at once blazoning it to the world? Fearless Fred wants not intellect or education; he would take steps, if he *did* possess such information, that you would soon hear of."

"True—true, Peter Bayley. You reason justly, and I feel easier than I did about this Fearless Fred. So now I will take leave of you with the thought that the—the——"

"Murder!"

"Well—well, the death of that girl is settled. I will tell the countess that all is arranged."

"For two thousand pounds."

"Yes, we understand each other. Farewell."

The earl left Peter Bayley alone, and then, notwithstanding the pain it gave the villain so to do, Bayley paced his room to and fro for about a quarter of an hour, during which space of time he did not utter one word. Then he flung himself into a chair and spoke—

"Yes, why should I hesitate? I have done worse deeds than that in my life— no, no, not worse—can there be a worse! But I have done as bad. These hands have already been dyed in blood. I have gone so far in the course that has shaped itself out to me, that to return is impossible, and so I may as well go on.— She shall die—yes, I will earn the two thousand pounds of this earl, and set his mind at rest, and then, too, if things should go wrong with me, as perchance they may, for of late I have noticed that some of the magistracy look but coldly upon me, I shall be able to call upon him to use all his interest in my behalf, and he must use it, knowing how fearful a secret of his I have in my possession. Yes, he must serve me; so, as well for that future consideration, as for the money now, and the hatred I bear to Fearless Fred, I will do it.

He returned to his chamber, flung himself upon his bed, and tried to sleep away the pains that were racking his limbs.

* * * *

It is time now that we look a little after Fearless Fred.

It will be recollected, then, that we left him to all appearance, in very good quarters, at the house of the kind-hearted and benevolent Mrs. Block.

Not only had that good lady succored poor Fred in his distress, and paid him every attention that his wounded condition required, but she had inquired into his state and condition in every way, and having learnt his.

"Strange eventful history," she had, with a philosophy and a humanity as rare as it is beautiful, determined, as if it were possible so to do, to rescue that bold spirit from the evils by which it was enthralled, and to make of Fred that which he possessed every qualification to become—a good and profitable member of society.

And yet there was a weight upon the soul of Fred that he could not account for. He had been left to sleep, and he had slept for a time, but his rest was disturbed by strange images; and while at one moment he pictured Jane in the power of the villain Bayley, at another he would start at the slightest noise, and fancy that he heard the stealthy sound of footsteps approaching to take him to a prison.

Probably the wound that Fred had received accounted in a great measure for these vagaries of the imagination.

But it will live in the recollection of the reader, that, although poor Fred did not know that such was the case, he had ample reason to feel faint and disturbed, and full of apprehension, for James the servant of the good and kind Mrs. Block, had formed the diabolical intention of giving up Fred to his foes.

The rascal was inflamed with the idea of making at once a considerable sum of money, by giving Fred into the hands of the authorities.

It must have been some sort of prescience of the danger that was thickening around him that made Fred so restless, as he strove in vain to repose himself in the house of Mrs. Block.

That lady was as good as her word to Fred. At first she thought of going herself to London at once, and doing what she could for him, but then she bethought herself that there was a Mr. Newcomb in one of the public offices, with whom she would like to consult first; not by any idea of taking his advice, as to whether or no she should befriend Fred—oh, no; upon that point she was quite decided—but he could tell her where the court then was, and the state of parties and affairs there.

The fact was, that Mrs. Block, in consequence of some early passages of her history, had a strong claim upon the gratitude of the Queen, and it was the Queen's interest with the king that she intended to use in the favor of Fearless Fred.

While James was making his arrangements to be off to London to betray Fred, Mrs. Block was writing the letter to Mr. Newcomb, requesting him to come to her forthwith, and thinking that she was taking the first step to save her young guest.

It was just as James was sneaking along the hall of the house to leave it, that Mrs. Block appeared at her parlor door with the letter in her hand, intending to call him.

"James," she said, "I have a letter that I want delivered in London. Do you know Whitehall?"

"Yes, ma'am."

"Very well. You will ask for the Home Office, and then deliver this letter to the gentleman to whom it is addressed. Do not spare any expense in getting to London, for this is a business I want settled as soon as it possibly can be."

"Thank you, ma'am. Perhaps I might as well go to the Unicorn Inn, and hire a horse."

"Do so."

In five minutes more, the treacherous servant was on his way to London.

At the close of the day, there was a loud knocking at the gate. Fearless Fred approached the window of his chamber, and pulling the curtain slightly aside, looked out to observe who it was that demanded admittance. His keen eye detected one man at the gate, and five others concealed behind a clump of trees, some few rods up the road. A glance was sufficient to inform the young highwayman that they were Bow street officers. In spite of himself, he trembled.

"What is the matter, Fred?" asked Mrs. Block, who was sewing at a little circular table. "Do you see any cause for alarm?"

Fred informed her of the state of affairs. The kind-hearted old lady started up, pale with terror.

"What is to be done?" she cried, wringing her hands.

"I have it," answered Fred, smiling. "You see, madam, that I am rather fair and youthful in the face, and about the same height of your servant. Now, I think if she would lend me one of her dresses, and a cap, that I could very well manage to elude the officers, even if they should come into the very house, and see me."

"Well, that is a chance that shall not be thrown away. We will see, then, if between us we cannot disguise you."

The girl was summoned, and made acquainted with the plan, in which she at once, with great good-nature, acquiesced, so that Fred was at once equipped, although, he wore the greater portion of his own clothing beneath the dress that the servant lent him. When his hair was parted in the middle, and a comb placed on each side, and a cap put upon his head, he looked so well, that Mrs. Block was astonished there could be such a metamorphosis, and but that he strode along in too masculine a manner in his dress, no one could, at a casual glance, have had any suspicions that he was any other than what he represented himself to be."

"If the officers do come, Mr. Fred," said the girl, "you must take short steps, you know, and not walk in that way."

"Trust me for that," said Fred. "I will act my part well enough, you may be assured."

"I do believe he will," said Mrs. Block; "but how does your arm and shoulder feel? I am much afraid that your wound will pain you."

"No. It is wonderfully better.—Youth is in my favor, I suppose, and a good constitution, for it is astonishing how soon I get the better of any hurt. I do believe that I shall soon be well."

The ring that a second time had struck upon their ears was a very sharp one, and Mrs. Block hastened to the garden to see who it was. Fearless Fred and the servant went after her; but not so closely as to make it seem that they had all gone to the gate together.

It was now rather dark, so that the garden was nearly a mass of shade, owing to the tall trees that were close to the gate; and it was but indistinctly that the figure of a man could be seen there.

"Is this Mrs. Block's?" he said, when she saw that lady approaching.

"Yes," she replied.

"Oh, then, I bring a letter from a gentleman in London for her, which he told me required an answer, if you will be so good as to give it to her. It is from a gentleman in the Treasury."

"What is his name?" said Mrs. Block.

"Well, it's on a card I have somewhere; but really I forgot it. It's—it's—Dear me, what is it? However, ma'am, if you will let me inside the gate, I will give the letter, if you please."

"You can easily give it to me over the gate."

"Oh, but that don't seem the right sort of thing, does it, now, ma'am? Ha! ha! That will do."

There was a sudden rush from the pathway leading to the back garden of some four or five men, and Mrs. Block, and the servant, and Fearless Fred, found themselves at once prisoners.

"Now," said one of the officers, "now, I think, we are all right."

"Alas! Alas!" added Mrs. Block, "has it come to this? All is lost!"

"Yes, you may say that," said the man. "Jackson, you keep an eye on these girls here, while you, Brown, look to the old lady. This isn't a bad un, is it, ma'am? You see, we wanted to keep you from giving the wink to Fearless Fred, for we know, bless you, as well as if we had him, that he is in the house somewhere."

These words at once had the effect of letting Fred and Mrs. Block and the servant know that he was completely unsuspected, and that his disguise had imposed upon the officers. Fred had a pretty good talent in disguising and altering his voice, but he thought it best to say nothing. The servant, however, told them that they were an unmanly set of wretches, and addressing Fred as Maria, she said—

"Don't you cry, Maria. I don't believe they will catch him even now, if they hunt for him ever so."

"He is not in the house," said Mrs. Block.

"No, ma'am, perhaps he's in the back garden, this time—ha! ha!" said the chief of the officers. "Come along, comrades, come, and seek the fox. We shall see whether these women are able to thwart us by giving an alarm to him."

"There's only need of one of us to stay here," growled the officer named Brown. "I'll look arter these female customers that they don't come after you, for that's all we need care about."

"Very well; you stay with them, and you, Jackson, come with me."

Jackson was the man at the gate, and when the other officers made their appearance, he had amused himself by kicking the door until he had broken it, so that the gate was swinging on its hinges. He and the rest of the officers, chuckling together on the prospect of speedily apprehending Fred, left the first gate to the care of Brown, who, when he was alone with, as he supposed, the three females, said, in what he intended to be quite a jocular tone of voice—

"Now, as for you two, my dears, who are young girls, I shall kiss the first one that tries to get away, and as for you, Mrs. Block, I shall put a pair of handcuffs on you, if you are at all troublesome."

"Oh, you are an ugly brute," said the servant.

"Am I? Ha! ha!"

"You are, indeed," said Fred, speaking in a capital female voice. "I only wish my young man was here, that's all, he'd soon settle you."

"Settle me, would he? Ha! ha!"

"Yes, he would; and I have a good mind to hit you myself, I have."

"Then why don't you? Ha! ha!— Hit me as hard as you can, my dear, and I won't say anything. I will only give you a kiss, mind you, if you don't knock me down. Do you think you could knock me down?"

"Yes, of course."

"Well, that's a pretty idea. Would you like to try? You shall, now, if you will agree that if you don't knock me down I may kiss you."

"So you may; but down you shall go," said Fred holding up his fist in such a ridiculous way, that Mr. Brown was quite delighted at the fun of the thing, and said—

"Hit away, now—hit away. No scratching, mind—I won't stand it."

"Oh, don't touch him, Maria," said Mary, "don't."

"No, my dear," said Mrs. Block, "you have no more strength than a cat. Don't touch him; you must be mad."

"Come—come," said Brown, "let the girl be. Fair play, you know, all the world over. If I like to allow her to hit me, what need you care? She can't hurt me, and I won't hurt her. Come on, my dear; you may try your best.— Come on."

"May I?"

"To be sure you may. There, now, you are getting frightened."

"Why, yes, you might hit me if you got into a passion."

"No! I tell you I won't."

"Very well, then you stand still.— Don't move, now, you ugly fellow. I don't suppose you will tumble far."

"Far? That is good. Ha! ha! Come, now, I want the kiss that I am to have afterwards, you know."

Fred advanced upon the officer, still holding up his clenched right hand in a manner that convinced Brown he had nothing to fear from its weight, but at the moment that he, Brown, was bursting out into another laugh at the fun of the thing, Fred threw himself into another attitude, and with the rapidity of thought, dealt Mr. Brown two such straightforward hits in the face that he was thoroughly bewildered; and then, before he could in any way recover or gasp out an alarm, another tremendous hit in the stomach sent him backwards, quite insensible, into a holly-bush, where he lay embedded, and to all appearance dead.

"That will do," said Fred. "Mrs. Block, farewell. I feel that to remain here any longer would be only to endanger you without saving myself. Farewell, and Heaven bless you."

As he spoke, Fred flung his arm round the neck of Mrs. Block, and kissed her, and then turning to Mary, he added—

"And you, too, Mary, I have much to thank for. Good-bye, and God bless you, too."

The kiss that Fred gave Mary came off capitally, and Mary, as she cried—"Well, I'm sure, what next?" did not seem very vexed at it.

"Stop—stop!" cried Mrs. Block.

Fred only waved his hand, and then darting out at the garden-gate, was in a few minutes quite lost in the darkness.

"Murder—murder!" shouted Mr. Brown. "Help! Oh, murder! The devil! Murder!"

We need not trouble our readers with a detail of what took place at Mrs. Block's after the departure of Fred. Suffice it to say that the officers were quite convinced Fred had given them the slip, and that, after some threatenings of what they would do with the old lady and her servant for aiding and assisting him, they left the house.

We now follow particularly the fortunes of Fred after he had disappeared from before the grieved eye of Mrs. Block.

The darkness was now so great that after getting a little way from the cottage he might fairly consider that he was safe from immediate pursuit, for it was quite out of the question that any one could take upon himself to say in which direction he had gone.

Still, Fred was not without an expectation that the officers would search the neighborhood for him, and so his idea was to get out of it as quickly as he possibly could.

With great speed he ran on past the few houses that were in the immediate vicinity of Mrs. Block's cottage, and then when he got to a part of the road which presented upon each side nothing but hedges, he managed, with some difficulty, to climb up and get into a meadow.

Having thus far, then, effected his escape, Fred thought he would stop and listen, with the hope of discovering if his foes were near at hand or not.

Lying flat upon the ground, he gave his whole attention to that idea, but he heard nothing. It was quite clear to him then that either the officers had not yet left Mrs. Block's garden, or that if they had, they had gone in a contrary direction to that which he had taken.

The former supposition was the correct one.

"And now," said Fred, as he partially raised himself and rested upon his arm, "and now, how do I stand, as regards my prospects and obligations. First, here I am, a lawless wanderer, without arms—without money—without food, and without a friend in the world whom I could choose to commit by going to.—Well, that is a pretty collection of withouts. Now, what else is there to think of? The police in search of me—a price set upon my head. Yes, that is about it —and—and ——"

Alas! there was something upon the mind of poor Fred that he would have put first in his list of troubles and anxieties, only that it was so great an anxiety that he dreaded to name it to himself even.

"Jane!" he at length managed to gasp out. "My poor Jane, where are you?"

This overpowering reflection, now, that he really and truly suffered his mind to dwell upon it, had such an effect upon Fred, that he sunk down amid the long damp grass, and there he lay for a long time as if death at last had smitten him.

Nothing but youth and its powerful principle of resistance to all depressions, whether physical or mental, could possibly have got Fred over the state into which he was cast by these sad thoughts of Jane; but he did recover, and, sitting up again, he murmured out—

"Oh, Heaven protect her! I am content to perish even now upon this spot, with no gentle voice to cheer me—with no friend to say 'God bless you,' when I close my eyes for ever, if she be saved."

It was the dreadful idea that she had fallen into the hands of Peter Bayley, that haunted poor Fred so bitterly, for as yet, he had no evidence that Bayley was killed or even dangerously hurt by the pistol shot that he had sent at his head with such good will.

In fact, reasoning from his own escape, he thought that nothing was more probable but that Bayley had been equally fortunate.

"What shall I do!" he now said.— "Oh, what can I do to aid you, Jane? Will not Heaven be good enough to point out to me some course of action now? for surely the cause that I would embark in is a holy one: it is the protection of innocence and simplicity against guilt and craft."

Fred had got thus far in this extemporaneous despondency, as we may call it, for it partook very much of the character of one, when he heard approaching horsemen in the road, on the other side of the hedge, and he paused to listen.

"I don't think it's a bit of use," said a voice, "but, however, I will keep guard here, if you like."

"Do so," said another voice, "and the discharge of one of your pistols will be a signal that you have made some discovery, and we shall be sure to hear it, and then we will all hurry from our posts to this spot."

Those voices were the voices of the officers.

"Ah," thought Fred, "so they are upon my track, are they? I must be careful."

He crept close to the hedge, and laid himself right under it in a dry furrow that was there, and which in wet weather was, no doubt, a watery course.

"I am certain," added the officer, who had last spoken, "that he cannot be far off. He is wounded, as we all know, and, besides, he has had no time to get to a distance, and if he be hiding, you know, all we have to do is to wait for daylight, and we must have him."

"A precious long time, that," said another.

"Not a bit of it."

"Yes, it is, though. It's a good eight hours now till daylight, and no mistake."

"Very well, all I can say is, that you are your own master in the matter, and

you can go or stay as you like; only when we do catch Fred there will be the more for them who are in at the last of it, if there are fewer to divide it among."

"Come, now; do go, Wilks," said another.

"I shan't."

"I thought you wouldn't old fellow; but don't let us have any bilking among ourselves. If we once begin upon that sort of thing, there is no saying where it will end."

"Oh, I don't want any grumbling," said Wilks. "Let's say no more about it. I'll keep watch here, till you send for me."

"That will do, all's right."

The others, upon this, walked off, and in a few moments, Fred heard the officer who remained, say to himself, as he thought—

"This is rather uncomfortable work, though, being out all night after the chap. What the deuce can have come of him, I wonder? I don't recollect having so much trouble after one of his trade before. Bother him, I only wish I could catch him, I should feel half inclined to take him to London alone, and bilk the others out of any of the rewards."

This seemed to the officer to be such a capital idea, that he quite chuckled over it again, and it reconciled him in a great measure to his lonely watch on the road. After a little time, then, he walked his horse for some distance off, and then returned, and so went to and fro, for the space of about a quarter of a minute only, from the spot so close to which was Fearless Fred, whom he would have been so delighted to capture.

"This won't do," said Fred. "It's perfectly true, as one of those fellows said, that if they wait till daylight they will have me as safe as possible. No—this won't do. I must be off before then."

The present danger offered to him, had the effect of enabling Fred to summon up all his energies again to the task of repelling it, and after a time he partly rose up, and tried to look through the hedge, to see what sort of man the officer was. The darkness was too intense, though, to enable him to do that; all he could see was the dim shadowy looking outlines of a man and a horse.

"If I had but arms," thought Fred, "I could face that fellow and then get away; but, alas! I have not. Well, I must try to cross the meadow, and see where that will lead me to, although, if they are occupying all the roads in the way they threatened, I may not much better myself by so doing."

But looking now carefully along the surface of the meadow, Fred felt quite confident that he saw a light in the distance, and that determined him, for he thought it possible enough it might proceed from some laborer's cottage, where there would be no disinclination to give him food and shelter for a little time.

There was no great risk in crossing the meadow so far as the officer was concerned, for it was too dark by a great deal for him to see Fred, and, besides, as each moment would increase the distance between them, of course Fred's safety was increased in proportion.

Gliding along, then, quite close to the ground, Fred got across the field to the opposite hedge, and then he saw that there was a kind of copse on the other side, and not a road of any sort, as he had expected.

After some deliberation, he resolved to proceed, although he had lost sight of the light which had been the original inducement for him to go in that direction. Crossing the hedge, he went through the trees of a young plantation for a little time, until he suddenly heard the barking of a dog.

Fred paused instantly.

The dog barked fiercely, and was evidently coming through the plantation towards him, and there was poor Fred, quite unarmed, and, consequently, unable to offer but a very slight resistance to the attack of the dog if it should make a rush upon him. Nevertheless, Fred waited, and prepared for the encounter as well as he could.

In the course of another moment the dog came bounding towards him, growling and barking.

"Down sir!" cried Fred.

This was answered by a growl, and the creature flew at him.

In the darkness, Fred had no means of seeing what sort of a dog it was, but he was soon engaged in a struggle with it for his life.

The first snap that the creature made at him fortunately only got hold of the cuff of his coat, and then finding which direction the dog's head was in, Fred tried the only thing that was in his power to do with any chance of effect, and that was, to lay hold of the animal's throat.

In a few moments Fred got his hands linked round the dog's neck, and nerved by desperation, he executed a pressure that under ordinary circumstances he would not have been able to do.

The dog made a choking sort of noise, and that encouraged Fred, who held still tighter each moment till he felt the creature hanging senseless from his hands. Giving the body a powerful swing then, Fred threw it right over the hedge into the meadow, and then, exhausted by the struggle, he fell to the ground himself, and lay for about ten minutes unable to move hand or foot.

Fred gradually recovered from this state, and to his great satisfaction, he felt that he had not suffered from the teeth of the ferocious dog.

"I will go on," he said. "Surely the people of the house—for there must be one near at hand—will not refuse to allow me to lie down and rest for a few hours. I must not tell them of the fate of this dog."

With this feeling, Fred made his way through the little plantation, till he came to some iron hurdles, which he clambered over, and then he found himself in a farm-yard. There was a cow-house close to him, and a glance within it showed him that there was a quantity of straw there; but he did not think that it was occupied by any animal.

Feeling very much fatigued, and feeling assured that if he were to attempt to go much further be would have to stop in some, perhaps, much less eligible spot than that he was now in, Fred went into the cow-house, and flung himself down among the straw in a moment.

When he was lying down he could hear by the breathing that a cow was in the place with him; but as he could not feel the creature by moving his hands about, he concluded that it was not near him at all.

"Ah," he said, in a low faint voice, "there is room enough for you and me both, cow, so I shall go to sleep."

With these words, Fred closed his eyes, and was fast asleep in half a minute.

It was very far from the nature of Fred to sleep very many hours in that place. He hoped that somewhere about the dawn of day he would be able to awaken; but it is very doubtful if he would have done so had it not been for the cow.

Fred dreamt that he was in a ship at sea, and that the crew were trying to roll him overboard, and when he woke up he found that a large brindled cow was pushing him with her nose and looking at him with surprise.

"Hilloa!" said Fred.

The cow made a noise as of pleasure to hear him speak, and Fred was glad even of the companionship of that poor beast at the time, and stretching out his hand, he patted it on the head.

"Well, cow," he said, "I suppose we must bid each other good-by, now, and thank you for a share of your lodging for the night, my good friend. You are more kind and humane, probably, than those who own you."

The loud crowing of a cock in the farm-yard without now attracted Fred's attention, and he rose and looked out from the cow's lodgings.

The morning was just commencing. Objects in the farm-yard were clearly visible, and a slight summer's rain was falling, which gave to the air such a freshness, that of itself it was quite a luxury to breathe it. A quantity of poultry had begun poking about in the yard for a morning meal, and some ducks were waddling off to a pond that was in one corner. No human being, though, was yet visible in the place.

"Breakfast, now," said Fred to himself, as he looked about him, "would be no bad thing."

At that moment he heard some one whistling, and a farmer's boy came into the yard. Fred did not think it prudent to hide; so he stepped forward at once, and spoke to the lad.

"Hilloa! Whose place is this, my good fellow? Can you tell me?"

No sooner had these words passed the lips of Fearless Fred, than the boy set up a shout of alarm, that might have been heard a mile off, and then he cried out—

"Here's one of 'em! oh here's one of 'em, master! Come and catch this one of 'em!"

"What do you mean?" said Fred.

"Master—master, here's one of 'em! Come and catch this one. Oh, murder! Here he is!"

These cries brought to the spot a thick-set, cross-grained looking man, who shouted out—

"What's all this about—hey?"

"There he is, master! That's one of the fellows. Don't you see him, master? Only look what an ill-looking wagabond he is, to be sure. Oh, he's one of 'em."

"Indeed!" said the man. "So, young fellow, I have caught you at last, have I?"

Fred shook his head, as he said-

"I wish I knew what you mean. I declare I do not."

"Oh, don't you? I daresay you are very innocent, my fine fellow; but we will soon alter your tone. What do you mean by being on my premises?"

"I am cold, hungry, and ill, and I

merely crept into the cow-house to sleep. I will go now."

"No you won't, though."

"Wherefore would you detain me? I have taken nothing from you; and after the specimen I have had of your temper, I shall go, asking nothing of you, although I am almost famishing. Farewell, sir."

"Oh, don't you think it You ain't going in that kind of way. Bill—Bill, I say!"

"Yes, master."

"Bring me that hay rope, yonder, and I will just tie the hands of this young spark behind him, and then you can take the cart-whip, and drive him to the cage."

"Yes, master."

"And do you think," said Fearless Fred, "that even ill, and weak, and wounded as I am, I will put up with such treatment?"

"Ah, we shall see—we shall soon see that, young fellow. You'll put up with it fast enough. Be quick, Bill."

"I'm a coming, master."

Fred was so indignant, that he looked at once about him, now, for some weapon of offence and defence, and observing a hay-fork close to the door of the cow-house, he caught it up, and exclaiming—"I'll teach you, you old ruffian, to talk to me in such a way," he dashed after the farmer.

Now, that British farmer was a very courageous man when he thought there was no danger, but so soon as he saw cause to come to a different opinion, he set up quite a howl of despair, and began to run off as fast as he could, pursued by Fred, who just caught him by the iron hurdles, and dealt him a rap on his thick skull with the fork that sent him rolling into the midst of a delightful muck-heap that there had been established for some time.

"Take that," said Fred, "you unfeeling brute."

The farmer was not an unfeeling brute, so far as the handle of the hay-fork was concerned, for he felt that, if he never felt anything in his life before, and he lay upon his back in the muck, looking so confounded, that it was not at all likely he would recover very quickly.

"Here's the rope, master!" cried Bill, suddenly rushing back. "Here's the rope, master. It's all right. You tie him up, and I'll drive him with the cart-whip to the cage, master."

"Will you?" said Fred.

"Oh, lor! Where's master?"

"I'll let you know in a moment," added Fred, and he charged with the hay-fork at Bill, who threw down the rope, set off at speed through the farmyard towards the house, and Fred followed him till they got to a fence, which Bill could not get over very quickly, so Fred gave him such a hoist with the hay-fork in the hinder part of his anatomy, that, with a yell that was enough to alarm the whole country, he made but one spring, and lit in a ditch over the other side of the fence in a moment.

"Well done Bill," said Fred.

It was quite clear, though, now, that after the manner in which he, Fred, had been met, and the sort of repayment he had given to that welcome, that he could not fairly expect anything at the farm-house, and, in fact, the best thing he could now possibly do, was to get away from it, as quickly as he possibly could.

The hay-fork, however, was too good a weapon to give up until he was quite certain that he was clear of his enemies, so he marched off with it in triumph, not hearing anything of either the farmer or Bill, who, no doubt were both under the impression that discretion was the better part of valor, and that if they said anything, he, Fred would salute them with another taste of the fork.

Nothing now seemed to Fred more probable than that he would soon fall into the hands of the officers, for it was getting lighter each moment, and he had a full expectation that they were still on the watch.

Darting under the iron hurdles, he made his way into the plantation, but he had not proceeded far before he met a laboring man with a stick and a bundle.

"Why, what's the matter!" said the man.

"Nothing. Do not impede me."

"Oh, I don't want, young fellow; but what has happened!"

"I don't know. All I want is to leave this inhospitable place, where, in lieu of a kind word or a morsel of victuals, I have been threatened by a man, who—but it don't matter. Good morning—good morning."

"Stop a bit. I'll be bound but you have come across Farmer Whitehead."

"I don't know, but his head let it be what color it may, is now in the muck-heap; for I knocked him down with the handle of this fork."

"You did? You have knocked down that old rascal Whitehead? You don't mean it!"

"Yes, I do; and there was a boy, too, of the name of Bill. I rather think he will remember me."

"Oh, that's better and better. Why, Whitehead is one of the biggest old scamps in the country; and that boy, Bill, is one of the most cruel, heartless, young rascals I ever came near. They have got a dog, too, that they call Bony, who bites everybody that he comes near, just for the love of doing so, I do think."

"Well, I throttled Bony last night."

"No!"

"Yes, I did. He attacked me, and it was the only way I could get rid of him."

"Give me thy hand, lad. Well, if I don't like to hear all that. Oh—oh! Old Whitehead in the muck-heap—and Bill poked with the fork—and Bony throttled! Oh! ha!—ha! Oh, dear! I shall laugh till I cry."

"Well, I shall leave you to your crying then," said Fred. "I'm glad you are so pleased at it."

"Stop! Don't go. Who are you!"

Fred was silent.

The man stepped closer to him, and then added in a lower tone—.

"There's been some officers searching every cottage for a highwayman. You can't be that, surely!"

"They accuse me."

"Do they? Well, never-mind Come with me, and you will be safe enough; for they won't come again, it's at all likely, after searching the cottage once. I'll be bound you want your breakfast, now, don't you?"

"I am faint and ill from wan't of food. I confess."

"Come along with me, then. But you are afraid to trust me, perhaps?"

"No—oh, no."

"Very well, then. Follow me close, and I'll lead you all right. Why, it's some mistake, surely. You can't be a highwayman; It's too bad."

"They want to take my life, though. It is Peter Bayley who has a grudge against me."

"The rascal! has he? Well, never mind, young fellow. You come along o' me, and I don't think they will find you in a hurry."

Fred was most grateful for this hearty succor. He cast away the hay-fork, and followed the laborer, who told him, as they went, that he worked for old Whitehead, who was so bad a master, that if he could get into any other farmer's service just then, he would leave him at once; but as employment was hard to be got at that season, and as he had a wife and child, he was glad even to take it from Whitehead.

At the termination of the plantation, there was a little woody lane, and some distance along that appeared a white-washed cottage, which, to be sure, looked miserable enough; but still, to the eye of Fearless Fred, it was most welcome, as a refuge against the officers who, for all he knew, aimed at his life to satisfy the villainy of Bayley.

"Here we are at home," said the laborer. "It ain't much of a place; but it keeps out wind and weather, for all that."

"It is very welcome to me."

"Well, and you are welcome to it, if it comes to that."

There was a little plot of garden ground in front of the cottage, and a little swinging gate just to shield it from the pathway of the lane. The commoner sort of vegetables only grew in the garden, with here and there a wild flower or two. Fred followed the laborer; and then when they got close to the door, a respectable enough looking woman came out, saying, as she did so, in a tone of surprise—

"What, back already, Robert? Is there naught for you to do at the farm?"

"Perhaps there is, wife, but I haven't been. I want you to give this young chap the best you have for a breakfast. Poor fellow, he wants it. Can't Bessy go for some more skim-milk to Robertson's?"

The Bessy alluded to was a fine, healthy-looking little girl of about seven years of age, and Fred could see her peeping from behind her mother at him.

"To be sure, Robert," said the good woman. "Come in, sir. Why, what has happened? Is it some accident Robert?"

"Shut the door—shut the door, wife, and I'll tell you all about it. There, now—put up the bar. Now, sir, you sit down, and don't you be afraid of them chaps. They won't come again."

"Oh, gracious," said the wife. "Do you mean the officers?"

"Tush!" cried the man. "I'll tell you all about it. Come this way, and I'll tell you while Bessy goes for the skim-milk."

The man soon satisfied his wife that Fred was a fit object for sympathy, and when she came back to him, she said—

"And did you really give that Bill a good progue with our hay-fork?"

"I believe I did. He howled loud enough."

"Then it was him that I heard all the way here, and I'm quite glad of it, for he is always ill-using animals; and only the other day he killed our poor cat."

"Cruelty to animals, madam," said Fred, "is one of those most unmistakable symptoms of a depraved disposition, which we are permitted to see, in order that we may never mistake the characters of certain individuals."

"Dear me, Robert," said the woman, "he speaks just like a book, he does."

"Yes," said Robert, in a low tone. "He is somebody, no doubt, who knows all that's in the old dictionary up stairs by heart. I have tried to read it through often, but never got beyond the second page, and then I was sure to fall fast asleep; but I daresay it is very interesting if one could but go on with it."

"No doubt of it, Robert. But do you think he would take a little of the pickled pork?"

"Yes," cried out Fred, "with great pleasure."

They did not think that he had over heard what they had been saying, and the woman quite started to hear him say what he did, while the man laughingly said—

"You see, wife, that young ears can hear sharply."

"Excuse me," said Fred, "I was not listening to what you were saying; but the words, pickled pork, struck upon my ears whether I would or not."

The woman now placed before Fred a very substantial breakfast, and the laborer departed to his work, at which he would be already sufficiently late to incur, no doubt, the great anger of the farmer.

"But, I don't mind that at all," said the man, "if I do but see a good lump on his thick head, and that, I have no doubt, I shall, for the hay-fork, if it be used with a will, don't hit very gently. So good morning, young sir, and be assured that you may remain here in perfect safety as long as you like to do so."

Fred warmly thanked the laborer for his kindness, and as Bessy brought back the skim-milk, he made by its aid, and that of the pickled pork beside, a very good breakfast.

There was plenty of sweet home-mad loaves, too, and although butter was luxury that was not to be had in t cottage, Fred did not miss it.

The good woman seemed to be quite delighted that her visitor made so good a repast; and when it was over, she brought him a large wooden bowl of clear spring water, with which he washed away all the traces of blood from his face, so that he looked quite a different being to what he had been, and the woman could not help looking at him with an eye of pity, as she said—

"And so, they want to make out that you are such a thing as a highwayman, do they?"

"Indeed, they do," said Fred.

"Why, it ain't in nature that you should be."

"And why not?" said Fred, with a smile.

"Oh, you can't possibly be wicked enough, I'm sure, with that face; so, if you were to tell me that you were a highwayman yourself, I don't think I should believe that such was the case, now, really."

"Do you want me to tell you?"

"Oh, no—no. Why, Bessy, child, what is the matter with you? Where have you been?"

Bessy had just rushed from the garden into the cottage with quite a scared look. For a few moments the girl could not speak, and when she did, she could only just manage to say, in alarmed accents—

"The wicked men are coming again, mother."

"Who?" cried Fred.

The woman ran to the door and took a look out, and then turning to Fred, while her face was very pale, she said—

"Are you afraid of the officers of police?"

"Yes."

She clasped her hands, then, as she added—

"They are coming. They are now getting over the gate which my husband must have fastened after him. Oh, what shall I do? Oh, what will become of us all!"

Fred rose and looked about him.—There did not seem to be the least chance of hiding himself there, and he said, with as much calmness as he could assume—

"Do not grieve for me. If they take me, it is no fault of yours, you know: for you can truly say that you do not know who I am, nor do you."

"Oh, no—no. But ——"

"Well, what would you say?"

"They will kill you."

"It is likely enough," said Fred, as he grasped the knife with which the pork had been cut. "They may do so; but it shall be at the peril of some of their own lives, for I am not one to sit still, and allow myself to be tamely slaughtered."

"Oh mother—mother!" cried Bessy, "I hear the men coming."

"What shall I do—oh, what shall I do?" said the woman, as she wrung her hands in grief and excitement.

"Nothing," said Fred.

"Yes, mother," said Bessy, "hide him."

"Where, my child—where?"

"Ay, that is the question," said Fred, looking round him at the cottage. "I fear me, that there are no hiding-places in such a place as this!"

"Oh, yes there is," said Bessy. "Don't you remember, mother, when I hid for fear from you and father, and you both looked all over the place, and couldn't find me?"

"Oh, yes—yes."

"It was in the copper, and some wet clothes upon me, so that you could not see me, you know."

"That is a chance," said Fred. "Where is the copper?"

"Here—this way," cried the woman.

"Oh, no, it is too late. They are even now at the door."

"The bar," said Bessy, as she adroitly put it in its place over the door. "They can't get in now."

A heavy blow was struck at the door, and the woman sunk half fainting into a chair. It was quite evident that she had not presence of mind enough to help Fred, or even to show him where the only place of refuge was; but Bessy placed her finger upon her lips, and beckoned him to follow her from the front room of the cottage.

The officers dealt another blow upon the door, as Fred followed his young guide, and she led him into a little kind of scullery, or wash-house, in one corner of which was the copper.

"Get in," she said.

Fred did not hesitate a moment. He felt that it was his only chance, and sprung in, and doubled himself up into as small a compass as he could, and Bessy threw a great quantity of wet clothes upon him, and shut the lid.

The officers were banging away at the door of the cottage now at a great rate, and Bessy called out to her mother—

"Open the door—open the door."

The mother did not move, so Bessy ran into the front room, and opened it herself, and a couple of officers made a dash into the cottage.

"How now?" said one. "What's the meaning of all this, eh?"

"Oh, yes, do tell us," said Bessy.

"What do you say?"

"That mother and me would like to know what's the meaning of all this, sir, that's all."

"Oh, would you? Now, ma'm, what's the matter with you?"

The woman was sitting upon the chair, into which she had fallen, looking as pale as death, and Bessy immediately said—

"The rat has gone now, mother. You needn't be afraid of it any more."

"The rat?" cried one of the officers. "What rat?"

"A large brown one, sir," replied Bessy. "They do, at times, come into the cottage, and mother is so frightened at them, she don't know whether to faint right away or not, I assure you, sir."

"Oh, indeed."

"Yes, sir."

"Don't keep on chattering to us, you little devil. Come, ma'am, where's Fearless Fred?"

The woman looked aghast.

"Fred who?" she said.

"Fred, the highwayman. One of our scouts says he saw somebody very like him come to this cottage with a man a little time ago."

"Oh, gracious!"

"Oh, it is—Oh, gracious! Come, where is he?"

"Why, mother," said Bessy, "this ugly man thinks father and brother Dick are bad people, surely, don't he? Oh, you horrid man, you are worse than any rat, I do declare."

"Hold your row! Come, ma'am, who was it that came here with a man?"

The laborer's wife by this time was recovering a little of her presence of mind, and she understood that Bessy wanted her to make the officers believe that she had a son who had come with her husband to the cottage, and been mistaken for the person they were in search of. It was quite a wonder, considering the fright she was in, that she was able to think so clearly at all as to be able to second Bessy's plan.

"Oh, dear, gentlemen," she said, "what has my Dick done?"

"Confound you and your Dick, too. It is Fearless Fred we want," cried the officer. "Come, where is he?"

"I don't know who you mean. My husband and my son have been here, and they have gone away again to their work; but that is all I know."

The officers looked at each other in doubt, and the one whispered to the other—

"Perhaps that stupid Brown has made a mistake, after all. What do you think?"

"It looks like it."

"Well, at any rate, let us search the cottage. If he is here, we shall soon nab him, for there can't be any hiding-place in such a place as this, I take it."

"Not one," said the other. "It would be ridiculous to attempt to hide here, I take it, unless he is up the chimney. That I will soon find out."

With this the officer took a pistol from his pocket, and approaching the chimney, he at once fired it up it, and brought down a volley of soot, that half blinded him.

"Curse the soot!"

"Well, laughed the other, "you are satisfied he is not there?"

"Satisfied! Yes, I am half blinded

besides being satisfied. Bother take it, who would have supposed a sack of soot was lodged there, and only waiting a touch to come all down at once?"

The officer who had escaped the avalanche of soot appeared to be highly delighted at his companion's misadventure, and could not contain his laughter at all, which put the other in a ten times worse humor than before, so that, drawing his cutlass, he swore that if he could only meet with Fred, he would at once run him through the body, and be saved all further trouble upon his account.

"Don't be rash," said the other.

"Oh, stuff! It's dead or alive, he is wanted by Peter, and nobody care which. We are authorized to kill him."

"We may kill him in self-defence, if you please; but not in cold-blood, if he gives himself up."

"Who is to know it? Let me ask you that. I say, who is to know it, stupid?"

"I will tell you. I am to know it, and, at a word, I won't have it done, so there's an end of it, and don't attempt it, now. Are you to go killing and slaying just because you happen to be in a passion? Oh, you needn't frown at me; I don't care for your black looks a fig."

The other growled out some oaths, and then he said—

"This is children's play. We don't come here to quarrel, but to find Fearless Fred, so let's drop the altercation, and come and look for him at once."

"With all my heart; but no killing just because some soot has come down the chimney into your eye."

"Oh! Bother you."

The mode of examination of the cottage was such, that if Fred had been hidden anywhere very accessible, he would, in all likelihood, have been very severely wounded, if not killed, for the officer who had drawn his cutlass thrust it rather carelessly into every hole and corner where it was possible any one could be stowed.

When they reached the wash-house, a glance round it showed them there was no place of concealment but the

copper, and that did not look as though it were big enough to hold even the slight figure of Fearless Fred.

"Confound him!" muttered the officer who was making so free with his cutlass; "he is not here, after all, and it must have been a mistake."

"I thought so from the first," said the other. "It didn't look likely."

"Well, it's only a little trouble."

"Yes, and a little soot."

The one with the cutlass lifted the lid of the copper, and looked in.

"Oh, clothes here," he said, as he gave a thrust downwards, with the cutlass; but in the position he had to use the weapon, he had but little power with it, and the point was entangled amongst the wet clothes. Throwing on the lid, then, with an emphasis that was enough to smash it, he said—

"Come on; it's no go."

"Not a bit of it," said the other. "I told you so."

"I say you didn't!"

"Ha! ha!"

"I say it's a lie—a—Well, well, I'm a fool, and that's the end of it. I didn't mean what I said."

"Very good. Now look you: this is the last time you and I go out together on any enterprise. You have no temper for your business, and you have only made one remark while in this cottage that has been at all correct."

"And what may that be?"

"Didn't you say you were a fool just now?"

The passionate officer bit his lip, but made no reply to this, and then they both passed out into the front room of the cottage, when he who had shown a calm temper, stepped up to the laborer's wife, and taking a pocket-book from his pocket, he said, in a cool, determined manner—

"Now, my good woman, did you ever possess fifty pounds in your life?"

"Fifty pounds?"

"Yes, it's a good round sum for the like of you, I take it; but did you ever possess as much?"

"Oh, no—no. I never saw such a sum of money as all that."

"Very well. You may not only see such a sum, but you may own it, too, if you will tell us where to lay our hands upon Fearless Fred. Here is a Bank of England note for the money at once."

"The Bank of England? Fifty pounds? Why, it's—it's—quite a little fortune—I mean, a great fortune."

"Well, it is something in that way. Can you give us the information where we can nab him, and take the note?"

The woman looked at Bessy, and gave a shudder, as she said—

"I don't know."

"Are you sure of that?"

"Oh, yes, of course. I wish I did. I don't know. It's a great deal of money, but as I don't know, I can't think of it."

"No go," said the officer to his companion. "He is not here. It is all a mistake. Come on."

They both walked from the cottage without another word, and the woman burst into tears, as she said—

"Oh, Bessy, only think—fifty pounds!"

"Yes, mother. But are you not as happy as a queen that you refused it?"

"Yes—yes. Thank God—thank God for that!"

Bessy mingled her warm and affectionate tears with those of her mother for some few minutes after the officers had left; and then turning to her child, with a smile, the mother said—

"Oh, Bessy! I feel as if I, too, had had an escape from death."

"From death, mother?"

"Ay, my child, from worse than death, for I did feel as if at one moment—it was only for a moment, though—that I would take the fifty pounds, and give him up."

"Oh, mother!"

"Nay, it was only for a moment.—The instant after I looked at you, and the sight of your face decided me the other way, and now I am so very happy."

"You are very good, mother, and you know that you could not give up the poor young man to death for a thousand pounds, no, nor for ten times that again; for what could have made us happy after such a thing as that? Would it not have been dreadful to get money in such a way as that?"

"Too dreadful! Every guinea would have seemed to be a drop of his blood."

Bessy shuddered.

"I will go and tell him now, mother, that the wicked men are gone."

"We will both go, my dear."

They both made their way into the wash-house, and Bessy eagerly removed the clothes from the copper, as she cried out—

"They are gone again, and you are quite safe. You can come out now, if you please."

"Help me," said Fred, and he spoke very faintly.

They were dreadfully alarmed to hear the tone of voice in which he addressed them, but they helped him out of the copper, and then they saw blood streaming down his neck, and Bessy uttered a scream of terror.

"Water," said Fred, "a little water. I am better now."

"But how is this?" said the woman, trembling as she spoke; "how did you get this hurt?"

"One of them thrust a cutlass into the copper, and the point of it gave me this gash in the neck. If I had staid much longer there I think I should have bled to death. I am not very strong now, as I have another wound to contend with. Heaven only knows what will become of me."

"My poor lad, they will kill you!"

"They are doing so, by degrees.—Thank you, Bessy, for saving me from them. I do think that they want to kill me."

"Only one of them," said Bessy, as she held the water for Fred to bathe his wound with, and cried at the same time, so that the tears coursed each other down her cheeks. "It was only one of them that wanted to kill you; the other one said that you should not be killed."

"It don't matter, one would have sufficed."

"But you are not dying now?"

"Oh, no—no; I shall be better now; and if they will only leave me alone now till nightfall, all will be yet well, I hope, with me, and I shall be able to go upon an enterprise which I hope to be successful in, before anything worse happens to me."

"Alas—alas!"

"Nay, do not cry for me, Bessy.— Who knows but I may yet escape all my enemies altogether! I am in rather a woeful plight just now, and my affairs don't look very promising."

"But tell me," said the woman, "are you the person that the officers really wanted? You may tell us now."

"I know I may: I am Fearless Fred."

A feeling of faintness came over Fred at this moment; the loss of blood and the excitement he had gone through were too much for him, and he fell off the chair upon which he had been sitting to the floor in a fainting fit.

"Oh, he is dead—he is dead!" screamed Bessy.

The mother was at first of the same opinion, and being a very timid woman, she was ready to faint herself at the idea, and was quite incapable of assisting Fred. It was at this moment, when she was holding by the little dresser in the wash-house for support, and Bessy was kneeling by the side of Fred on the floor, that they heard a footstep.

"Oh, God, they are coming again!" cried the woman.

Bessy screamed and clapped her hands over her face, for if Fred were not dead quite, she fully expected to see him killed before her eyes in the next minute.

The sound of the approaching footstep came nearer and nearer, and then the door of the wash-house was pushed open, and a voice said—

"Where are you all?"

It was the voice of the laborer himself, and with a cry of joy his wife sprung forward to meet him.

"Oh, Robert—Robert, they have killed him!"

"Good God, no!"

"Yes—oh, yes; look at him."

Bessy now sobbed convulsively, and the poor man was thoroughly bewildered for a few moments among them.

"Gracious Heaven!" he said, "I did not expect this. Some one told me that two men had been here, and I came home then as fast as I could. But you do not mean to tell me that they have murdered this youth?"

"Yes—oh, yes!"

"And he is Fearless Fred," said Bessy.

"Poor fellow, I suspected it," said the man. "I thought as much from the first. But it is a sad end for him to come to surely. Are you sure he is dead?"

"Look at him."

"Well—well, poor fellow, he does look dead enough, to be sure. Did they shoot him?"

"No—no."

The laborer bent over Fred, and then he said suddenly, as he placed his hand upon his heart—

"Why, he is not dead."

"Not dead?" shrieked both Bessy and her mother.

"Now do be a little quiet both of you, and bring me some cold water and some vinegar, if you have any. I tell you he is no more dead than we are; he has fainted, that is all, and will, no doubt, soon come to himself again poor fellow. Why, you must be both out of your senses."

"We have been so frightened."

"Oh, stuff! The water Bessy."

"Yes, father, and here is the vinegar."

Bessy watched the operation of restoring Fred to consciousness with an absorbing interest, and when she saw him, after about five minutes, fairly open his eyes, she clapped her hands with joy, and called out—

"Oh, there are his eyes again, that I thought we should never see more.— Look at his eyes, mother!"

"Hush, my dear—hush!" said the father. "He must be kept quiet; rest will do him more good than anything else, and we ought to get a doctor to him."

"To be sure we ought, and we will too."

Fred was sufficiently restored to hear these words, and he shook his head in disapprobation of them, and then he managed to say very faintly, but still sufficiently distinctly for them to hear him and fully to understand him—

"No—no; only rest, nothing but rest. No doctor."

"Very well," said the man, "it shall be so. You may depend, wife, that he knows best. I will carry him into the front room, and place him upon our bed, poor fellow, and then, perhaps, he will go to sleep."

"Sleep!" said Fred. "Oh, yes, it is sleep will save me now. I feel very weak and heavy."

It was, no doubt, the loss of blood that made him feel so inclined for sleep; but so it was, he could hardly keep his eyes open, so they carried him into the front room, and laid him on their humble bed ; and not expecting that it was at all likely the officers would make him another visit to the cottage, they permitted him to rest where he was in peace. In a few moments a deep slumber came over poor Fred.

The poor man and his wife were now in the greatest possible perplexity to know what to do. They found that Fred was very much injured, and that when he should awake he would be much worse than he was then, and they looked at each other, thoroughly bewildered to know what to do.

"What shall we do?" said the wife.

"I know not," said the husband.

"Why, take care of him, to be sure," said Bessy. "He can't eat a great deal, and he can have my dinner, you know, every day, and I'll do very well upon my breakfast and supper ; besides, I can get lots of fruit from Mr. Smith's orchard, for the gardner will give me whatever I ask for. If it were the blackberry time of the year, too, I shouldwant for nothing."

"You know not what you speak about," said the husband. "But we must trust to Providence in the matter, and take things as they fall out. Give him up to his enemies, I will not."

"That's my own father," said Bessy.

The wife did nothing but cry, for she foresaw, or she fancied she did, the breaking up of her humble home, all through this most unfortunate adventure. And yet she knew not how to avoid it, so she cried still more, the more she thought over it, and was quite incapable of giving any advice, or of adopting any rational course upon the occasion.

The laborer did not leave the cottage, seeing how completely helpless his wife was, and so the day wore on, and no living soul came to that humble abode to disturb the slumbers of poor Fred.

Probably sleep did more for Fred in regard to his wounds that the most skillful surgeon could have accomplished.— Nature has modes of restoration of her own of which, after all, with all our boasted science, we know but little ; but certain it is, that the sleep, or the cold-water bandages, or both together, had the effect of very much restoring Fearless Fred to a better state than one would have supposed to be possible.

When he opened his eyes, the cottage was very dark indeed, and for a few minutes he could not take upon himself to say exactly where he was.

Bessy and her mother were by the fire-side conversing together in a low tone of voice, and Fred as he lay there still, by them supposed to be asleep, heard plainly enough what they said to each other.

The fire-light now and then lent a flickering and uncertain glow to the little room when a flame started up from the consuming embers ; but that was not often.

"Ah, my dear," said the good woman, "you know that I would do anything in the world for this poor youth who has been cast upon our kindness, so don't suppose that by what I have said I repine at the consequences, or think of doing him any harm, Bessy. I would not for worlds."

"I know that, mother," said Bessy, and she evidently spoke through her tears.

"Well, my dear, don't cry."

"No, I won't, if I can help it, mother. But you really don't think that anybody would be so wicked as to turn us out of our humble little home just because we did an act of kindness to this poor Fearless Fred."

"Hush! my dear, hush! Let me beg of you not to pronounce his name. There's danger in the very sound of it. I will not say that I regret his coming here, for I do think that if he had not he would have by this time been with the dead; but I cannot help feeling the danger we run by harboring him."

"What can we do, mother?"

"Nothing, my dear—nothing. I would not let him know for the world that I thought as I did. I wonder what it is that detains your father?"

"Yes, he is late."

"Suppose we go out into the lane, then, and watch for him, my dear? I am so full of apprehensions, that I really cannot stay in the house."

"Come, then, mother. We will go at once. I suppose he will not awaken yet?"

Bessy approached the bed, but Fearless Fred closed his eyes and imitated a deep and tranquil sleep, so she stepped lightly away from him, and with her mother left the cottage.

The moment they were both gone Fred sat up in the bed, and was well pleased to find that his head was better than it had been, and that his strength generally was very much recovered by the rest he had had.

"I will not stay here," he said, "to bring distress and danger upon these poor people. Let what may be my fate, I will not involve them in it. I will leave them at once, and seek my fate far away from this cottage home. They shall not have to say that it was through me they were made houseless wanderers upon the face of the earth."

Fred rather tottered when he got fairly to his feet, for a slight sensation of giddiness came over him; but he knew that that would pass away soon, so he did not heed it in the least, but

looked about for his boots, which had been taken off.

Fred was soon ready to start here, then, after one more glance round the cottage he went to the wash-house, and got out at its little window, and so into the back garden, and then by climbing a stile he was in the open fields again in a minute or two.

He turned and cast one last look at the cottage, and then, as he said, "Farewell," he struck across the meadow he was in at as much speed as he could command.

But Fred was not now proceeding at random through the country. He had made a determination which, if he could only carry out, might, at all events, have the effect of very much altering the situation of Jane, whatever might be his own prospects in consequence.

"I will proceed at once," he said, "to the place which Jane described to me as that wherein she had hidden the cedar-box, and I will not rest until I have fully ascertained its contents; and if they should suffice to clear up the mystery of her birth, I will then, heedless of my own position, proceed to London, any place the papers in the hands of some one who will, from his official position, be bound to see justice done to her."

CHAPTER XI.

FRED FINDS THE CEDAR-BOX, AND UN-
RAVELS A GREAT MYSTERY.

FRED, notwithstanding all that had occurred to him since he had left Mrs. Block's house, was still not very far from it; so that he had a very tolerable comprehension of the road that he ought to take.

At that hour of the evening, though, when each moment the outlines of objects were becoming more and more confused, it was no easy matter to say exactly which was his nearest course to take; so, he went on with the hope that he would get to a high road, and possibly, then, be able to ask his way to the spot, which was in the immediate neighborhood of Finchley.

With this resolution, he walked in as straight a line as he could, crossing the hedges as he went, when suddenly, just as he found his way through one, a rough voice called out—

"Who goes there?"

Fred drew back, and did not answer, so the voice repeated the question in still more peremptory accents, and Fred thought it best to answer.

"A friend," he said. "Who are you?"

"Come forward, then, if you are a friend, and don't be skulking behind a hedge. If you want to know who I am, I can tell you that I am a Bow-street officer."

"Oh, indeed!"

"Well, come on. I am on duty here, and must examine all suspicious persons, you know."

"What! Do you mean to call me a suspicious character?"

"To be sure I do."

"Then I shall certainly not come forward after such an insult as that. A suspicious person, indeed! I am surprised at your confounded impertinence, Mr. Officer."

"Stand, or I fire!"

"Fire away!"

"Ah! is that your game? You are, perhaps, the very person we want, for he is not over particular about a pistol-shot or two, so I shall have you."

"When you catch me," said Fred as he ran along the hedge at a swift pace. He heard the officer breaking through the hedge; but he was evidently in doubt as to the course that Fred had taken, for at first he ran some distance across the field, and then he called out in a much louder voice—

"Hilloa, my young fellow! If it's all right, only say so, and I shan't waste my time in running after you."

This was only a *ruse* by which he might hear the sound of Fred's voice, and so know in which direction to pursue him; and Fred, considering it to be such, very wisely held his tongue.

"Why don't you answer?" cried the officer.

Still Fred was silent, nor would he move now till the officer did so, and drowned the sound of his footsteps with his own.

"I'll have you, if I die for it!" muttered the officer, and he made a dash towards the hedge, now, and Fred thought that it was high time to get out of the way.

Close to the bank upon which the hedge grew, he found a small gap, which was just about *large* enough for him to force himself gently through, and by its aid he reached the by-road upon which the officer had been stationed. Not knowing, then, very well whether it would be better for him to turn to the right or to the left, in order to proceed on his destination, and yet feeling that to delay was the most dangerous thing he could possibly do, Fred took the right-hand route, and ran on quickly till he saw something in his way, which in the darkness he could not at first make out at all.

Pausing to take a good look at the object, Fred then saw that it was a horse tied by the bridle to a branch of a tree that happened to bend low enough for that purpose, so that it could be very well reached by any one upon the horse's back.

"That this was the officer's horse Fred did not entertain a doubt for a moment; and when he felt the holsters by the side of the saddle, and the stocks of the pistols in them, he was quite confirmed in the idea.

"This is a lucky chance, indeed," said Fred, as he sprang upon the back of the horse.

At that moment he heard footsteps just over the hedge in the meadow, and he knew that the officer was close at hand, then, and that the sound of the horse's feet would at once let him know what had happened.

"Woa!" cried the officer, trying to

look through the hedge at his horse to ascertain that it was all safe.

Fred stooped down upon the saddle, so that his head should not be seen, and probably all would have been well, but that the clatter of horse's feet in the lane, from some approaching horseman suddenly became manifest.

That the person who was approaching was another officer, was but too probable, and Fred did not feel inclined to wait the result of the encounter upon that spot. Slipping the bridle of the steed he had appropriated off the bough of the tree, he set off at a gallop, but without saying a word, so that the officers might, if they were so inclined, think that the creature had broken loose, and merely run away from impatience of having been retained so long.

"Hilloa! Stop!" cried the advancing horseman. "Stop, I say, Jones. Where the devil are you going?"

"I'm here," said Jones, from the other side of the hedge. "It's my horse that has run away, I'm afraid, Mr. Lee."

"Well, if he has, then, he has run away with some one on his back, for I saw that much, at all events."

"The deuce you did?"

"Indeed I did, whether it is the deuce or not."

"It's Fearless Fred, then, as I'm a sinner!"

"Fearless Fred, do you say?"

"Oh, lor, yes. I thought it was that fellow. I got over here to hunt him out, and he has played the double upon me, and gone and taken possession of my horse. Here's a pretty situation. Oh, I could knock my own head off."

"Then I shall leave you to do it at your leisure," said the other, as putting spurs to his horse he set off at full gallop after Fred along the lane.

Now this officer was rather better mounted than Fred, but yet the latter had about two minutes the start of him, and that, with a horse at speed, is no small matter. The officer probably felt that, for he fired one of his pistols as a signal to any of his comrades who might

be about, to let them know that he was in pursuit of Fred, and then he spurred forward at his utmost speed, and Fred heard him coming fast up with him.

"Hurrah!" cried another voice from a cross-road. "Hurrah! we have him now."

"The deuce take it," said Fred, "they will stop me now, I fancy. Well, we will see what sort of weapons there are in the holsters."

With a pistol, now, in each hand, and the reins in his teeth, Fred dashed on, and at a point where another lane intersected the one he was in, a mounted man made a dash at the bridle of his horse, but failed in catching it.

"Try again," said Fred.

"Who are you?" cried the man; but Fred was twenty yards in advance before the words were well out of the officer's mouth.

The sharp report, now, of a couple of pistols after him, smote upon Fred's ears, and he felt a strange sensation in the left shoulder, as if a sudden blow had been struck at him.

"I am hit," said Fred, as he turned in the saddle and fired one of his pistols along the lane.

With what effect or with none, he had fired, he could not tell, for he galloped on at once, and then another shot was sent after him, and on the moment the horse fell, and Fred was pitched over his head into the middle of the lane.

Luckily, Fred had kept hold of the reins, and they saved him, in a great measure, from the consequences of the fall. He was on his feet again in a moment, and standing by the dead body of the horse, for the shot had killed it.

Flight, just at that moment, was out of the question, for the pursuing horseman was too close upon him, so Fred took up a position by the side of the body of the horse, with the other holster pistol in his right hand.

"Surrender!" cried the advancing horseman, as he brought his steed to a stand. "Surrender, Fearless Fred!"

"Wait a bit," said Fred.

"I'll ride you down, if you don't give in at once."

"Try it?"

"Confound you, then, here goes."

The man spurred his horse against Fred and his dead steed, but Fred crouched down, and the animal made a clean leap over them both. Fred rose again, as he cried out—

"Your horse is better bred than you are. Try it again."

"No, I won't try that again, but I'll try that."

As he spoke, he fired a pistol at Fred, and hit him in the cheek, inflicting a gash through it, but not by any means a dangerous wound, although Fred, at the moment, thought that it was serious.

"Coward," he said. "You have but a sorry victory. May my death lie heavy on your soul."

"Ha! ha!" laughed the officer. "we won't trouble ourselves about that."

Poor Fred stood bewildered for a moment or two, and quite forgot the pistol that he held in his hand, till the officer cried out—

"Come, now, you know you are hit. and if you have any fire-arms about you, you had better fling them down, or I will treat you to another bullet."

"Thank you," said Fred, as he dropped on one knee. "Now look out for yourselves."

"Hold! Don't be a fool."

"Oh, no, not at all. Look out."

The officer crouched down upon his saddle, and spurred his horse to desperation, but the animal was frightened, and began to rear so, that Fred had a tolerable fair mark to fire at. Bang! went the well-rammed-down pistol, with a stunning report, and the officer fell, with a loud cry from his saddle, and the horse started off at full speed dragging him along by one foot, which was entangled in the stirrup.

Fred was alone.

"I am killed, I suppose," said Fred, as he fell upon the dead body of the horse. "Oh, Jane—Jane, if I could but have lived a little longer for your sake!"

Fred lay still for the space of about ten minutes, fully believing that his last hour had come; but then a feeling came over him that, after all, it might be possible for him, wounded as he was, to reach the spot where the cedar-box was hidden.

"Oh, if I could only crawl there, at the cost of any amount of suffering," he said, "and if it could be found by some one in my grasp, even when I was dead, all might be well with Jane."

This idea roused him to make every possible exertion, and he rose, and tottered along the lane. The wound in his shoulder gave him the most pain, now; but he could guess that the wound in the cheek, and the blood that had poured down him, must give him a very ghastly look, and yet, each step that he now took he gathered hope, for he found that the weakness he had felt did not grow upon him, and that was everything.

"I shall yet do it," he cried. "Oh, yes, I shall yet, perhaps, be able to save Jane. If I could but do something to those rights of which she is so unjustly deprived, before I die, I should be able to render up my last breath to Heaven with scarce a pang."

It is astonishing how some strong mental resolve will at once, and completely overcome great physical depression. It was so with Fred, for there is very little doubt but that if he had not been so intent upon securing the cedar-box and its contents for Jane, he would have died from loss of blood and exhaustion in the lane.

Now, however, so sadly wounded as he was, he ran on until the lane entered a high road, and he paused to look about him, to see if he knew the spot.

There were two tall trees not far from him. One was a poplar, and the other sycamore, and at the foot of the latter there was a little well of spring-water, the pleasant bubbling of which over the sides of a rude earthern basin that had been constructed to hold a supply of it at all times, free from impurities, came plainly upon Fred's ears.

With a sudden cry of joy, he fell to

the earth by the side of the spring, and then he just found words to say—

"It is the place! This is the place described by Jane. Oh, kind Heaven! surely I have been brought here to save her."

It was some minutes, now, before Fearless Fred recovered from the sudden surprise and the shock of joy that had come over him, and then amid the gloom he looked at the trees again, and said, in a soft low tone—

"Oh, yes—two trees—one a poplar, and the other a sycamore, and a spring among their roots. They call the spring 'The Old Saints' Well,' too, she told me. Ah! some one comes. Who is this? I am unarmed and at the mercy of my enemies, now. I have but a small knife that I brought from Mrs. Block's."

The footsteps that he had heard approached rapidly, and then he heard some one whistling, and he saw by the height of the person and gait, that it was a boy—

Fred now wished to make assurance doubly sure, for he had a lurking fear that imagination might be deceiving him, and making him think he had found the spot he sought, while he might yet be far from it, so he called to the boy.

"Hilloa, my lad! Hilloa, there!"

"What is it, master?" said the boy.

"What do they call this spring?"

"The Old Saints' Well, sir."

"Thank you—thank you. Oh, what blessed words! It is—it is the place. I will save you, Jane, now."

The boy had passed on, and Fred was alone again.

But Fred had now made up his mind to a course of action which not all the world could have by any possibility turned him from, and he, with at the moment a pardonable superstition, looked upon his presence at that spot a something like a direct evidence of the approval of providence to the course which he intended to pursue from that time forth.

"I will save Jane," he repeated, "or I will perish in the attempt!"

So clearly and so minutely had Jane detailed to Fred where she had hidden the little cedar-box, that there could not be the most remote possibility of a mistake in the matter.

If by no chance the ground had been disturbed at the spot, then the box would to a certainty be where she had so prudently and with so much forethought for its preservation placed it.

"This is the spring," said Fred, as he sat down beside it, "and this is the tree she spoke of."

A draught of clear water from the spring seemed to him to be perfectly delicious, and to renovate his strength most wonderfully; but probably his delight at having reached that spot, which he had so ardently desired to have the opportunity of reaching, had more to do with the renovation of his strength and his spirits than the draught of water he had taken, although we are by no means inclined to depreciate the many good qualities of clear water.

But to return to Fred.

His great care now was to feel quite sure that no one was at all near him to watch his actions, for if any one had seen him, the supposition would, without doubt, be that he was seeking for some hidden treasure which he knew to be in that spot, and he would then very probably have a contest yet for the possession of the cedar-box.

Fred was in no good condition to do battle with any one at that time, so his great object was to avoid any such necessity, if he possibly could.

A very few moments sufficed to convince him that, in good truth, he was alone there; and then he commenced his search beneath the old tree.

Oh, what anxious moments they were, during which, with such inefficient means as he possessed for such an object, Fred disturbed the grass and mould away from the roots of the old tree. At one moment he was the prey of all the anguish of despair, as a conviction seemed to shoot across him that the box he so much sought was not there; at another a ray of hope crossed his heart as he told himself how likely it was that he should find it at once.

"No—no," he said. "Why should I expect to be so very fortunate as to hit upon the exact spot in which she placed the box? I will still search, and I will not give up hope."

And he extended his researches round the old tree; but he began soon to despair again, and he was upon the point of giving up the search as useless, when his hand touched something that was within a portion of the roots of the tree by a stone.

"It is here—it is here!" he cried.

With incredible rapidity, now, Fred cleared aside the rubbish, and in another moment he held the little cedar-box in his hands.

"Yes, there was the cedar-box that Peter Bayley had risked his life more than once to get possession of. There was the box, which the earl would have given a good thousand pounds at any hour to have had but a glance at. There was the box, which had been the cause of so much persecution to Fearless Fred whom Peter Bayley thought the knowledge of where it was hidden might be extracted from, and which, no doubt, had saved his life upon more than one occasion, from the dread of Peter Bayley, that if Fred were dead the secret of where it was hidden would die with him.

Wounded, weak, and exhausted, Fred held it in his hands, and hugged it to his heart.

"It is a treasure," he cried, "which may yet have the effect of saving Jane. I feel that I ought not now for a moment to doubt its importance to her and her fortunes. It was but my dread that I should not find it, which made me for a moment or two try to delude myself with the idea that it was, perchance, of but little value to her. It is a treasure —a treasure, and now for London."

"Halves!" cried a rough voice, and from among the trees close at hand a man sprang out.

Fred was upon his feet in a moment.

"What do you mean?"

"Halves, young fellow, that's all.— You have found something in that hole at the foot of the tree and I cry halves.

That is fair, all the world over, as you know."

"Idiot!"

"Come, come, you had better keep a civil tongue in your head, or I may take all. What is it?"

"What is that to you?"

"Oh, I'll soon let you know what it is to me. It is money, of course, young fellow, and that is everything to me. Come, now, don't be a fool, or else I shall not be very particular about giving you a crack on the head, and taking it all."

"You!" said Fred. "Why, you are not armed."

"Am I not? Perhaps you didn't notice this little blackthorn twig that I have in my hand—Ha! ha! I rather believe that a tap with it, young fellow, will settle all disputes between us."

"I shouldn't wonder," said Fred; and then maddened at the idea of the possibility of having the cedar-box wrested from him after all the trouble he had taken to possess himself of it, he felt as if animated by the strength of ten men, and with a fierce cry he sprang upon the man like a tiger upon its prey, and so sudden, and so utterly unexpected was the attack, that Fred had the blackthorn stick out of the fellow's hand, and had brought it down with such a swinging blow upon his head, that it was awful to hear it.

The man fell as if struck by lightning.

"For Jane! For Jane!" cried Fred; and still holding the stick in his hand, he started off at a mad pace along the road.

Not far, however, had Fred gone, with the stick in one hand and the cedar-box clasped in his breast by the aid of the other, when he heard voices calling out loudly—

"Stop him—stop him! There he goes—stop him!"

Frightened with the idea that his enemies were upon his track again, Fred made a dart at a bank by the road-side, and breaking through a hedge at the top of it, he fell a considerable height into a field, and struck his head against a plough that had been placed just under the hedge on the field-side.

For a moment Fred tried to rise, and then everything seemed to swim round with him, and he fell back again insensible to the ground, still clutching the cedar-box, although the stick that had done him such good service had fallen from his hands in his fall.

How long he lay in this state of insensibility poor Fred had no possible means of knowing, but he was awakened by water splashing in his face, and when he opened his eyes he knew not where he was for a time.

All was perfectly dark around him.—There was a dull heavy pain in his head, and he was devoured by fever, so that the water that fell upon his parched lips and skin was quite a boon.

As recollection slowly returned, he heard a howling wind around him, and the sough of it in the tree tops as it careered over the fields and through the hedge-rows. Then he found that he was lying in a field, and that he was soaked by rain, which was still coming down in a fearful torrent.

"The box," he gasped, "the cedar-box!"

A gleam of joy shot across his heart: he had the box still safely in his grasp, although his fingers were quite benumbed by the tenacity with which he had held it for so long.

"I have it," he said, "I have it still, and that is everything. How long have I lain here? Oh, Heaven, has cruel fortune not punished me enough now? Shall I never be able to reach London with this box? I never had such ill fortune as this when I was engaged in deeds that were wrong and indefensible; but now that I have determined upon changing my very existence to do some good, I am thwarted and frustrated at every turn. Oh, help me—help me, Heaven, for the sake of that young and innocent being whom I wish to save."

Fred found that he was a little better and stronger after this strange, brief and half-complaining prayer, and as fancy goes a long way towards fulfilling in reality its suggestions, there is no doubt but that he was really better.

The rain still came down in perfect torrents, and the wind at times swept by in such impetuous gusts, that it would seem as if it would be impossible for the strongest trees to withstand its violence for much longer.

A water course that was close to Fred, and which ran along by the roots of the old trees and bushes in the hedge-row, had increased to a perfect torrent, and roared and bubbled on its way with all the importance of a little river.

"It is night," said Fred, "and what a night—ano yet what is it to me, if I did but know where I was? My head is better. The rain is doing wonders for me in allaying the fever that was consuming me. I must rise and find my way to London for your sake, Jane."

Poor Fred found that every joint in his body was terribly stiff when he tried to rise to his feet, and that made him suspect that he had been lying a long while in the field under the hedge-row.

It was only by dint of stamping upon the ground and moving to and fro in the field for some ten minutes or so, that Fred at all succeeded in restoring his joints to anything like freedom of action, for until he had done so he did not like to attempt to cross the hedge at the risk of another fall into the road, which might disable him again.

Oh, what would he not have given then for a sufficient light to enable him to open the cedar-box and look at its contents! He had an idea that it would be better to take the papers from it and conceal them about him, but he could not see to do so where he was, and he dreaded to drop the smallest fragment of them in the field.

"No—no," he said, "I will run no risks. Who shall say that I might not lose the most important document of all that the box may contain? I will keep it intact until I have light wherewith to look well at its contents."

With this determination, Fred placed the box within both his coat and waistcoat, and although it pressed rather uneasily upon his chest, he buttoned his coat over it, and felt content that he had it.

The box, with its supposed precious contents, was like a talisman to Fearless Fred, and appeared capable of lifting him far above all petty evils.

Having gained the roadway now, all he hoped was that some one would speedily pass of whom he might inquire which way he ought to turn his face to reach London, but in such a night as this, and at such an hour, for it was late, it seemed rather a doubtful thing that he should meet anybody at all.

"I must husband my strength," said Fred to himself. "If I take half a dozen steps only in the wrong direction, those half dozen steps will have to be retraced, and that makes a dozen, so I will sit upon the bank here, and wait until some one passes."

Fred felt very weak and ill, notwithstanding the artificial kind of courage by which he was upheld, and as he sat upon the bank, and the rain poured down upon him, he could not help some of the most melancholy reflections concerning his situation coming over him.

"All," he said—"all my visions of happiness with poor dear Jane seem now to have flown to the wind. Here am I, a harmless, weak, and wounded wanderer, by the way-side, not knowing which way to turn even to brave the dangers that beset my path, and with no information as to whether poor Jane be dead or alive."

The idea that it was possible Peter Bayley, instigated by the earl, might have taken the life of Jane, sent such a bewildering pang to the heart of poor Fred, that it nearly prostrated him where he was, and there is very little doubt but that if the least confirmation of such a notion had come to him, but that he would have given up even life itself along with hope. But Fred was yet in his early youth, and it is not at such a time that despair has power to linger long around the heart, or in the chambers of the brain.

For a time, it is possible enough that the depressing effect of combating circumstances may be greater in youth than in men advanced in years; but the spring-like power of action is also greater; and youth rallies from difficulties and depressions which would utterly and for ever, prostrate age.

So was it with our friend Fred.

By the time he had sat for some quarter of an hour upon the bank, and listened to the wind and the rain, he almost smiled as he said—

"Ah, no, Heaven never made such a being as Jane, to be the victim of such a man as Peter Bayley. No—no, I won't, and I can't believe that such is possible. Oh, if I could only look now at what is in this box! Ah, some one comes surely, or is it but the patter of the rain in some puddle in the road?"

Fred had thought that he had heard the sound of a footstep, nor was he mistaken, for a few moments afterwards he heard the sound more plainly again, and then he heard the lowing of a cow, and a voice.

"Get along with you, do. Here is a pretty night's work I have had to find you, and no end of damage to pay for you, you wretch—all owing to your straying over to old Mr. Smith's pasture, you obstinate beast, when you have a paddock of your own, and as comfortable a dry shed, on such nights as these, as any cow would wish to have."

The cow came splashing along, and the crack of a stick now and then upon the hind quarters of the animal, showed that her master was in anything but a good humor, or disposed to spare her on account of her contrary propensities.

"Here," thought Fred, "is an opportunity of asking my way, which, will not, probably, occur again; so I will go out into the road, and speak to this man."

Keeping his left arm firmly clasped over the box, which he had placed so close to his heart, Fred stepped out into the middle of the road, and called out, in as cheerful a voice as he could assume—

"Am I going all right for London?"

"How do I know?" said he that,

"when it is so dark. I can't see which way you are going; but I have no doubt you will stop my cow.

"No, I wont; I will get close to the hedge, and let her pass. It is a very rough right."

"Well, it is. Get on, will you? The way to London is behind me and the cow, that is to say, we are both coming from that direction, and just at the turn of the road, you will see a sign-post. No, you won't, though, for you would need to have the eyes of a dozen cats to see anything on such a night as this.

"Thank you," said Fred. "Good-night."

"But you ain't going to walk to London, though, such a night as this, are you?" said the man.

"Yes—yes. I must reach London, and there is no conveyance."

"Why, its eight miles."

"So far? Alas! I fear I am hardly able to walk it; but I must try. Good-night, and thank you."

"Well, but the mail-coach will be up in about twenty minutes, if you like to wait for it, and it will put you down in Oxford-street in less time than you can walk a quarter of the way."

"Indeed? Will it surely pass here?"

"Yes, to be sure. It always does."

"Thank you—thank you. I will sit here and wait for it."

Fred, as he spoke, felt in his pocket to assure himself that he had not lost some money that Mrs. Block had given to him, and then he made up his mind to avail himself of the mail-coach; for the idea of his walking eight miles in his present state was, he felt, out of the question.

"But you don't mean to say that you will wait in the rain?" said the man.

"Oh, yes—yes. I have nowhere else to wait."

"Come to my cottage, or rather, I ought to say, my dairy, for dairy it is that I keep. It is only a little further on, and its no great odds you know, whether the mail picks you up a little on one side or the other of this spot. Fol-'ow me and the cow. You may as well be under shelter for twenty minutes as not."

"I thank you," said Fred; "and perhaps you have got a light, too, in your cottage. Is it not so?"

"A light? To be sure. Why, you don't suppose, do you, that I and my wife sit in the dark, hardly, all the night! However, I can tell you, we wouldn't be up at this time, only that we had lost our cow, and we could not possibly think where she had gone, till it struck me about half an hour ago that it was as likely as possible she was in old Smith's ten-acre field."

"And there you found her?"

"To be sure I did. Of course. You know old Smith?"

"Indeed I do not."

"Well, I did think that everybody knew him; but it don't matter. So, come on at once, for I'm wet through, and I daresay you are quite as bad."

"Are you sure we shall hear the coach?"

"Oh, yes. I'll put a light in the window, and when the guard sees that, he will guess it is some one who wants to go by it, and he will blow his horn so you will be all right."

"I am much beholden to you."

"Don't mention that. Can you see the cow?"

"Yes, faintly."

"That will do, then. All you have to do is to keep her in sight, and you can't go away, and we shall be housed in a minute."

Fred could just see the bulky object which had the dim resemblance to a cow before him, and he followed along the road till the man called out—

"Here's the gate. Come right on."

A very few moments were sufficient now to take Fred into the parlor of a little snug cottage that was by the road-side. A piece of turf was smouldering away upon the hearth, by the aid of which the cow-keeper soon lit a candle; and then, as the light irradiated the little cottage, he, for the first time had a good look at his guest.

"Good gracious!" he said.

"What is the matter?" said Fred.

"Why, who are you! Oh, lor!"

"Am I so frightful?"

"I don't know what you would be if you were soaped and cleaned a little; but you do certainly now look as though you had been through all the ditches in the parish, and you are all over blood, too. Why, what has happened to you to make you in such a state?"

"I have been ill-used," said Fred, faintly.

"And robbed?"

"Oh, yes. And robbed. But I have a little money still left; and if you will sell me a drop of milk and a bit of bread, I shall not only pay you cheerfully, but be very much obliged to you beside."

"I'll call my wife."

"Nay, do not do that. Recollect how fast the time is going. I shall have to go in another ten minutes."

"That's true. Here's some new milk, and here's plenty of bread. Stop a bit. I'll beat up some new-laid eggs in the milk for you, and that will do you most good. But who are you?"

"Alas! I am an unfortunate being: but will you pardon me for being so rude as to look if my papers are all right, while you are so kind as to get me the milk and eggs?"

"To be sure. Do just as you like here."

With eager and trembling fingers, Fred took the cedar-box from beneath his coat, and began to untie the tape that fastened it.

"Now," he thought, "at length the secrets of this box will be known to me."

The dairyman proceeded to beat up the eggs for Fred in the milk, and he, Fred, soon got the cedar-box open. It was quite full of papers; but the uppermost one was watered to the lid, partially, and had upon it these words:—

"If, upon the sudden death of Lolanti, this box and its contents should fall into the hands of any one inclined to do an act of great justice, let him take it at once to some high legal authority, and placing it in such hands, demand that tardy justice should at length be done to the oppressed."

"Yes, I will!" cried Fred.

"Eh?" said the dairyman.

"Nothing—oh, nothing."

"Dear me! I thought you were taken suddenly ill."

"Oh, no—no, my good friend. I was only speaking to myself, that was all. I am very anxious concerning my papers, you perceive, that is all. Pray, do not heed me, my good sir."

"Oh, very well."

With trembling eagerness, Fred laid his hands upon a folded paper that lay next to the one he had read, and after casting his eye over it for a few moments, he sprang to his feet, crying—

"The coach—the coach! Where is it? Oh, why does it not come at once, and convey me to London? Jane! Jane! you will be saved—you will be rich and great—oh, God! and I shall be the means of making you so—my own very beautiful Jane!"

"He's mad," said the dairyman, as he caught up a large milk pail, and held it before him, in an attitude of defence.— "Keep off now—don't—don't—Lie down, poor fellow, do."

"Very good, sir."

"Lie down! Come—come, look, at my eyes. Down with you! Be good, now, will you?"

"I am not mad, I assure you."

"Of course not. I did not expect for a moment that you would own to it, but mind, I haven't done anything to you —keep off!"

"Why will you persist in such a delusion? I assure you that the exclamations I uttered merely had some reference to a discovery I had made by reading one of these papers. It is a discovery that has filled me with joy. Indeed, I am as sane as you are, I assure you."

"Are you quite sure of that?"

"Quite," said Fred, with a smile.

"Well, I don't think you do look quite so mad now; but you rather alarmed me. However, here's your eggs ana milk. It is a wonder that I did not upset them all in my fright."

"Thank you—thank you. In a moment."

Fred hastily, but securely, tied up the cedar-box again, and secured it in its former position beneath his coat; and then he eagerly partook of the eggs and the milk, which he hoped would give him strength to proceed to London, and do what he had to do in Jane's cause.

"Many thanks," said Fred, as he took some money from his pocket. "You have done me a great favor."

"Oh, never mind about paying. That will do another time, and there is the mail-coach. Hark! don't you hear the tread of the horses' feet?"

"I do—I do. Oh, stop it for me. I would not miss it for a thousand pounds. Stop it for me, I beg of you. I am too weak to call out loud enough, I fear."

The mail-coach with its four horses, came dashing on; but the dairyman reached the door of his cottage in time to call out, "Hoi!" in such a tone that if the coach had been a mile off, his voice would surely have reached it.

The coach pulled up.

"A gentleman for London," cried Fred.

"All's right, sir," said the guard.— "Inside?"

"No, out. It's a fine night."

"A fine night, sir? Why, it's a pouring, and has been for these six hours past or more."

"I like it," said Fred, as he climbed up to the outside of the coach, where there was not a single passenger besides.

"Well, my eye!" said the guard, "there's no accounting for tastes. All's right, Bill."

"Kim up," said the coachman, from the recesses of about half a dozen handkerchiefs that was round his neck, and off started the mail-coach again, at a good ten miles an hour for London."

Fred could not help having a vivid recollection of the remarks which the man at the dairy had made upon his personal appearance, and he blessed his stars that the night was so dark a one that the guard of the mail-coach could not have the slightest idea of the condition of the passenger the vehicle had been stopped to take up.

There can be no question but that if the guard had seen him, he would have met the offer of such a passenger by a most decided negative; for certainly never was any naturally well-looking person in so truly awful a plight as was poor Fred upon that occasion.

What with the blood from the wound in his head, and the mire from the road and the bank, and the field, and the rain which had washed all that down his unfortunate face in long streaks, he looked as abject a wretch as the imagination can possibly picture.

But what did he care? His heart was lighter now than it had been for a long time. He had the cedar-box in perfect safety, and he knew the secret of its contents—that secret which will soon now be known likewise to the reader; and if he could only have been quite sure that Jane still lived, he would have sung for joy.

But, notwithstanding all his arguments to the contrary, the dread notion that Jane might have been murdered by Peter, would at times come across him, and chill his very heart. Vehemently and steadily, however, had Fred held that supposition at arms-length, for he felt that if he only began once seriously to entertain it, that it would soon lay hold of his imagination and crush him with the mental agony it would inflict upon him.

The coach dashed on through mud and through rain upon its way, and very soon the lights of the great city began to be visible to the scrutinizing eyes of Fearless Fred.

It was then that Fred, covering his face with his hands so as to shut out external objects, gave himself up to thought for a short time as to the best manner in which he could obey the injunctions of that paper which had evidently been written by Lolanti.

"Yes," said Fred, "I feel that that advice or that command, call it which I may, is good, and I will carry it out, let it cost me personally what it may. I will take this cedar-box and its contents even as it is, and even as I am, to some great personage, upon whom shall rest the responsibility of acting upon their contents."

The sound of the horn of the guard of the coach, as the vehicle rattled through the northern suburbs of London, now recalled Fred to considerations of the present rather than the future.

Looking around him, he saw that the coach was close upon the long, straggling thoroughfare of Tottenham-court-road, then but very partially built upon, and to the left as you came into town quite open to fields.

The coach dashed on and turned into Oxford-street, where the lights of the street were more numerous, and Fred felt that a discovery of his wretched plight must be soon made.

The inn-yard into which the coach would enter now loomed upon his sight, with a glare of light just within it.

Poor Fred would have given anything in his power to get out of the glare of the great lamp in the inn gateway, but that was impossible. If he had made an attempt to leave the coach, it is ten to one but that, as it was going at a tolerable speed, he would have met with a severe fall, and possibly have done himself so much injury as to interfere with his plans regarding the cedar-box and its contents.

"I must evade the questions and the remarks," he said, to himself, "of all those who choose to make them."

With a rattle and a dash the coach entered the inn-yard, and as ill luck would have it, the coachman drew up so exactly under the light of the lamp, that the full rays were thrown on to the roof, and exhibited the squalid mud-bedaggled figure of poor Fred.

"Now, sir," said the guard, "I hope you are not very wet? Hilloa! hoi! why what the d—l is this?"

"What's the row, Ben?" said the coachman speaking from amid the folds of all his handkerchiefs, and wrappers, and coats.

"Why, look here Bill, what a pretty passenger we picked up on the road. By George, it's some scarecrow from a wheatfield."

"Oh, I'm blowed!" said the coachman.

"What is your fare?" said Fred.

"Our fare? Oh, lor! Why, our fare is half-a-crown, but you haven't got it, that's clear enough."

"There it is."

"A bad 'un, of course."

"You scoundrel!" said Fred. "If I was not better engaged, I would make you repent this insolence. The money is good. Take it, and beware how you and I encounter each other another time, when I have leisure and inclination to punish insolence."

Fred flung the half-crown on to the pavement of the inn-yard, and sprang to the ground at the same moment.

A man with a pipe in his mouth came to the door of the inn at the moment of Fred's alighting, and, in fact, Fred came close to his very feet.

"What's all this?" said the man.— Hilloa! Stop! Murder! Help! This is Fearless Fred, the highwayman! Hold him! Stop him!"

Fred sent the officer, for it was in truth one, reeling against the wall with one well-directed blow, and then he dashed out of the inn-yard before any one could venture to stop him.

Luckily for our poor friend Fred, the streets at that hour—for it was half past eleven o'clock at night—were tolerably slack of passengers; another hour, and they would be fuller, for then the theatres and the taverns would have given forth their contents; but as it was, there were not many persons to stand in the way of even such a fugitive as Fearless Fred, and especially was that the case as regarded the west-end of the town, to which he was directing his hasty steps as best he might upon his mission.

He heard the shout behind him of

"Stop him—stop thief!" That awful cry to the poor wretch who feel that it is levelled at him, and that he is hunted by his fellow-creatures from street to street, and that in every one he meets he sees but a foe.

Fred dashed wildly, but not altogether unthinkingly, on, for he took a route that he had determined upon as he sat on the coach top amid all the soaking rain.

It was to the residence of the Lord Chancellor of England that Fearless Fred the highwayman, upon whose head there was set a price, wended his way with pursuers at his heels.

Now, the Lord Chancellor of that period resided in Piccadilly in a large house nearly facing the upper or western end of the Green Park, and it so happened that on that night he gave a grand entertainment to the judges and other personages connected with the courts of law and judication of the kingdom.

So much legal wisdom had scarcely ever before been collected together beneath one roof as that night could have here produced beneath the Lord Chancellor's.

————

CHAPTER XII.

DANGEROUS CONDITION OF JANE.

WE feel compelled, notwithstanding the exceedingly critical position in which we leave poor Fred, to repair to Newgate street, for the purpose of glancing at the condition of Jane, whom we have been scarcely able to think of while following the varied course of Fred since the time when, wounded and insensible, he lost her upon the road.

Probably the greatest safeguard that Jane experienced in her situation of prison in the house of Peter Bayley consisted in the fact that the woman, or mistress, of the thief-taker, regarded the poor girl in the light of a rival, who would eventually supplant her in the affections of Bayley, and therefore hated and persecuted her with all the venom of a low and brutally passionate mind. The creature had even gone so far as to attempt the life of the unhappy Jane, who, from that moment, instinctively trembled at the bare presence of Mrs. Popham, as her persecutor was called throughout the thief-taker's establishment. This attempt upon the life of Jane, was prevented, at the critical moment, by no less a personage than Peter Bailey himself, who, from that hour, looked upon himself as, in some measure, the young girl's defender, and for better security, from the malignancy of his old and jealous mistress, removed Jane from the habitable part of the house, to one of the many cells which formed the underground portion of the miscreant's establishment. This removal of the fair object of her jealousy, inflamed the jealous fury of the old hag to a still higher pitch; and she spent the greater part of her time in poudering over the means by which she could reach and destroy the unhappy Jane.

The frightful compact between Peter Bayley and the Earl of Broughton for the murder of Jane still remained intact in both their minds, and the reader can easily conceive that they were not exactly the sort of men to alter their determination in cases where any rascality was concerned.

It had been agreed on that Jane should be violently sent upon her pilgrimage to another and a better world than this upon the next night but one to that upon which such a consummation of the persecution which she had endured had been resolved upon.

Jane little suspected that to the apprehension of the earl and of Peter Bayley her hours were numbered; on the contrary, the part which Bayley had taken upon the occasion of the attack of Mrs. Popham upon her had tended to impress her with the belief that no personal injury was intended her, but that any means would be resorted to to induce her to make the disclosures that were so much wished by the earl.

Of course, the principal secret she had

to keep consisted in the fact of where she had hidden the cedar-box, and if Bayley could only have convinced her that Fearless Fred was dead, she would not further have hesitated to tell all she knew, for then she would have felt that life for her had lost all hope, and that all she had to look for would be that species of severity which is after all but a mockery of happiness, but which time generally vouchsafes to the most wretched.

It is now the afternoon of the second day—the day anterior to the night when the Earl of Broughton is to come with his two thousand pounds to Peter Bayley, and upon which occasion he is to see the deed done which is for ever to rid him of Jane.

Why he so ardently desired to be rid of Jane the reader has already a suspicion; but all that will be made clear very shortly.

And now it will hardly be believed, considering who and what Peter Bayley was, and knowing how pitiless—how absolutely fiend-like in its remorselessness his course had been, that he began to shrink from the performance of the deed which the night coming was to witness, if all things happened according to arrangement between him and the earl.

We can offer but two reasons for this unaccountable weakness upon the part of Peter Bayley.

In the first place, then, the youth and beauty of Jane had had an effect even upon the flinty heart of that man of many crimes, which proved that even he had left some faint remnants of human feeling in his bosom.

It would seem to be impossible for any human being to exist at all, and be utterly dead to all feelings.

That, then, was one of the reasons of Bayley's timid shrinking from the murder of Jane. The other was, perhaps, one that he did not himself understand, and that he never for a moment suspected. It consisted in the fact that he had defended her from Mrs. Popham; and it is a principle of human nature that what we defend and protect we are much inclined to continue defending and protecting.

Hence, then, was it that Bayley, if any other mode of keeping faith with the earl, and of earning the sum of money he had been promised for the deed, would have been glad to spare Jane.

The afternoon deepened into evening, and yet there were many hours between then and midnight, when the wicked earl was to come to Newgate Street and claim the performance of the dreadful contract, so that Peter had time to think.

Having quite recovered sufficiently from his hurts to be in much his usual state, Bayley sat in his private room in deep thought.

"What can I do," he muttered, " to save the girl? If I could only cheat that rascal Broughton, all would be well. I must think of some method of doing so. Who knows, though, but that the girl may relent yet? I have a great mind at the risk even of being more weakened in my resolution than I am, to visit her again, and by what I can do to persuade her to purchase life and liberty by telling where the cedar-box is to be found. By Heaven! if she does tell, Broughton shall not have her life."

With this determination, Bayley rose and abruptly opened the door of his room. Mrs. Popham was immediately outside.

"What do you do here?" growled Bayley.

"What's that to you?"

"Ah! is that the game you are going to play? Are you not afraid to speak to me in that way?"

"No, I ain't ; and for half a pin, I'd go to Mr. Sheriff Watkins, and tell him all about his plate, and how you kept it till you thought the reward enough to make it worth your while to give it up ; and if I do, you know as well as I do that you will be hanged, Peter."

"Indeed."

"Yes, you have enemies."

"And friends, too, my sweet Mrs. Popham. The secretary of state finds me too useful in taking political prisoners to make an end of me. How many Jacobites, now, do you think *I* have laid hold of ?"

"I don't care ; but you shan't bully and bluster at me. I know what you are at well enough."

"What ?"

"Oh, forsooth, you ugly old beast, you must take a fancy to that child who is in the cells. Do you think I have no eyes in my head ?"

"Two, Mrs. Popham, and they both squint dreadfully."

"Wretch !"

"Ha! ha! My dear woman, go to your comforter—your rum or your brandy. I don't know which delightful compound it is, now, that you give the preference to ; but I can assure you that you are a most amiable woman when you are so drunk that you can neither stand, walk, nor speak."

"Never mind that. I'll have that girl's life yet."

"Will you, indeed ?"

"Yes I have sworn it. She shall die by my hands. I don't want any of your pink faced, grey-eyed children brought here with their arms and growls, not I; and, I tell you, I will dispose of her.'

"We shall see to it."

"Yes, we sha'n't, Peter; and I know you are going to her now. It is no use of your trying to deceive me. You are going to meet her now, the little vixen, I know you are."

"For once in a way," said Bayley, as he sorted his keys to get hold of the master one that opened all the locks in the house, "you are right, my dear Mrs. Popham. I am going to visit Jane."

"Oh, I shall expire!"

"As soon as you like. Don't let me hinder you, madam. I can only say that I shall do my very best to survive such a calamity, and to bear it with resignation."

Mrs. Popham seemed for a few moments to be meditating a spring upon Bayley, to avenge herself upon him for his conduct; but prudence and recollection came to her aid, and prevented her. She had tried before that mode of settling their little differences, and had come off rather the second best in the affray, for Bayley was not very particular.

"Very well," he said, with a forced calmness. "Wait a little—wait a little, that's all."

Bayely laughed scornfully as he walked down the long narrow passage that led to the cells. But although in presence of Mrs. Popham, Baily laughed, and affected to make light of her threats, he did not do so to his mind; and as he closed the door at the end of the long passage after him, and descended the flight of stone stairs leading to the lower regions of the house, he muttered in rather anxious tones—

"That woman knows quite enough to be very dangerous if she chooses to be so. If I only thought that she really meditated any mischief, I would take care that it would need to be her ghost that carried it out, if it were carried out at all, for she should not, in this world, have the opportunity of so doing."

Bayley took good care to secure the numerous doors behind him as he went to the cells, and taking then a small oil lamp, which burnt with a sickly and uncertain radiance upon a niche in the wall, he soon reached the long, damp, narrow passage from where opened the cells that he had, in defiance of all authority, or all right, had constructed in connexion with his house; thus, at once, converting it into a prison, where he, from his own personal feelings, might immure any one

without a shadow of law or justice to favor the act.

"Now," said Bayley, "if I can but persuade her to make a clean breast of it, and to tell me all that the earl so much wishes to know, she shall not be sacrificed, poor young thing, for that would be a pity. I will try her again about Fred's death. Let me consider. What shall I say to her upon that head? Oh, I have it."

Bayley advanced to the door of the cell, and listened for a few moments. He heard a low, soft, moaning voice, and then he shook in every limb.

Jane was praying.

The coward color forsook the cheeks of that bold, bad man as he heard the name of God pronounced by the lips of that innocent young girl, and, with a deep groan, Peter Bayley dropped upon his knees at the iron door of the cell.

As Bayley sunk to his knees upon the cold, damp floor outside Jane's cell, she began to sing in a low, sweet, plaintive voice, the verse of a psalm that she had learnt when she was quite a little girl.

The tones were so sweet, and now and then so broken by sobs, and the words were so simple and innocent an appeal to that Divinity who loves innocence and simplicity, that Bayley felt as if at that moment he were about to choke. He soon recovered his equanimity, however, and rising, he turned the lock, entered the cell, and placed the lamp upon the floor. It cast a strange light upon his hideous features, which were still covered with plasters.

"I heard you speaking just now," he said. "What were you saying?"

"I was only praying."

"Praying? Oh, that won't do you much good. But it's a matter of taste, so we needn't quarrel about that. Come now, you want fresh air, and light, and sunshine, and flowers, and you would like to hear the songs of birds, and the rippling of streams, and all that sort of thing, would you not?"

"Oh, Heaven, yes. Why do you, in this place, agonize my heart by reminding me that there are such things? This is a refinement upon cruelty."

"No. I want you to enjoy all that I make mention of. You are young, and pretty, as they say angels are. Well, I make war upon men, not upon such as you are. I want to let you go, and so, as you said you would not tell me whether Fearless Fred lived, I have busied myself in finding out whether he really was alive or dead."

Jane looked at him with staring eyes.

"Now," she said, "you are going to try to kill me by the relation of some dreadful story, but I will not believe it,"

"Well, that you can do as you like about. I tell you he is no more, and you shall see his dead body."

"No—no!"

"Oh, well, if you won't, you won't, but it's the only way I have of convincing you of the fact, if you won't take my word for it. Will you believe me, then, that he is dead?"

Jane shuddered.

"His last words," added Bayley, "were addressed to you. We could hardly hear him, for the blood, hot and frothy as it was, was welling up in his throat, and the doctor said that if he went on speaking he wouldn't live a minute."

Jane started, and covered her face with her hands, as if by so doing she could shut out all perception of the dreadful image which Peter Bayley brought before her mind's eye.

Bayley saw the effect he was producing, and he continued—

"But he would speak, for all that, though he was half choked each time that he tried. He would speak. I suppose, because it was of you he wished to speak before he died."

"False!—false!"

"As you please," said Bayley, biting his lips. "You can believe it, or not, as you like. In the result it matters not one straw to me. I will tell you, partly, because it is for your own good, and partly that I promised him at his last gasp that I would do so, and I am a man of my word."

"If he be dead, you killed him."

"No, Jane; there you do me an injustice. The fact is, I tried to save him."

"You?"

"Yes, you doubt it; but you will believe me when I tell you that it was not from any affection to him, or from any feeling of humanity, but just because his life would have answered some of my purposes better than his death.'

"Go on—go on. Tell me all."

"I will," added the wily thief-taker. "Finding at his last moments that I pitied him, he said, 'If you should find Jane, tell her it was my last request that she no longer endangers her peace and safety from any fancied expectation that she will benefit herself by keeping the secret of where the cedar-box is hidden—tell her to give it up, and then to leave England, and try to seek a home and a subsistence in some foreign land?'"

"I told him that if it were any consola-

tion to him in his last moments to know as much, that you were in my custody, and that I would faithfully report his words to you, and I told him further that I would give you a hundred pounds to expedite your journey from England, so that you should not be, cast upon a foreign shore in a state of destitution. As I told him this, he died."

Jane was like one stunned. The thief-taker observed her with a triumphant smile.

"Think the matter over," he said. "I will come back to you in an hour, and by then you had better be ready to give me an answer."

With these words, Bayley left the cell, and Jane heard the harsh grating sound of the locks that he closed after him as he repaired to the more habitable portion of his house.

"It is not true!" she said. "The hollow deception spoke its own worthlessness in every word he uttered. It is not true! Fred lives yet! He is not dead! But what will become of me? I am here friendless and alone, and threatened with death.. Oh, Heaven, have mercy upon me, and spare me from death in this frightful place!"

A slight tapping noise against the wall of the cell at this moment attracted the attention of Jane, and she held her hand to her ear to listen to the sound. It came again, and more distinctly than before.

"What can it be?" she said. "Oh, what can it be? Is it some new horror that Bayley is preparing for me in this place?"

She scarcely dared to utter these words, even in a whisper, to her own heart, so terrified was she each moment becoming, for the tapping sound rather increased than diminished.

Suddenly, there was a rustling sound like the fall of a quantity of loose earth and rubbish, and then Jane was startled by the glare of a light, and looking up, she saw a hand passed through a hole in the wall, and holding a little bit of wax taper in it, which burnt dimly in that wretched atmosphere.

"Help!—oh, help!" cried Jane. "What is this? Oh, have mercy upon me!"

"What's the row?" said a voice. "Don't be bellering out in that way, my dear. I suppose you are the little pretty girl who they want to get rid. Is your name Jane?"

"It is—it is."

"And did you live in the old conjuring crib along of Lolanti?"

"Yes—oh, yes."

"And Fearless Fred is your fancy, ain't he?"

"Fearless Fred? Oh, tell me what you can of him, and I will thank you with all my heart. Tell me that he is not dead, and I will bless you!"

"Dead? Who said he was?"

"Bayley."

"Stuff! he's no more dead than I am.— He's worth a precious lot of dead 'uns yet, I'll be bound."

Jane burst into tears, and she wept with joy, as she cried—

"He lives! he lives! All is well yet, for my Fred lives!"

"Go it," said the voice. "You keep up that roaring while I set to work again. But I say, Miss Jane, couldn't you hold this little bit of a light, and cry at the same time? It would help me, and I don't think it would be any hindrance to you—only don't be crying into the snuff of the candle, for, so sure as you do, you'll put it out."

"But who are you?"

"Nibbling Joe."

"Who do you say?"

"Nibbling Joe, my dear. Lor bless you, did you never hear of me? Well, this is prime, arter all! Why, my dear, I'm the most out-and-out chap at grabbing a wipe—fumbling for a quid, or playing the double with a ticker, or coming any dodge as you can name, as never was: and you never heerd of me?"

"No, Mr. Nibble, I never, indeed, heard of you."

"Well, that's a rum un. Why, my dear, they calls me Nibbling Joe on account of my professional pursuit, in a way of speaking, you know. But hold the light a little higher, and I'll soon have down some of old Peter's wall here, and then we will see if we can't give him the go-by."

"Oh, is there any hope?"

"Well, I own Peter holds rather hard when he gets his hand on a fellow, but I mean to try it, and no mistake. Keep out of the way, Jane, for I am going to push through a bit of the wall on that side. Now for it. There you go, and here am I all right. I look upon this as half-way to getting the better of old Peter."

A mass of about two feet square of the wall was now broken down, and Nibbling Joe, who was one of the most famous pick-pockets of that time, crawled into the cell in the occupation of Jane. The young girl held the light in her trembling grasp, and she saw a rather pleasing but effeminate person-age in Nibbling Joe, who, shaking the dust and mortar of the wall from his apparel, looked rather earnestly at her.

"And so," he said, "that rascal Peter has had the villany to shut you up here just to please the Earl of Broughton?"

"The Earl of Broughton!" said Jane.— "Is that the name of my persecutor?"

"Yes, and a plague to the name, I say, for it was that name, and nothing else in the world, that brought me in one of these cells."

"But are you sure of the identity of such a nobleman with the man who has been my foe?"

"Quite. He is tall, and rather stout, with a full complexion, and thick lips, gray eyes, and partially bald?"

"Yes—yes. The same. But how could it concern you?"

"Just because I was foolish enough to interfere in other folks' affairs. I saw him come to Bayley, and I knew him, and by putting one circumstance to another, I found out that he was Bayley's employer about you, and I thought it a sad thing that a young creature such as you are, should be sacrificed to a rascal like that, and I foolishly said as much to Bayley, and uttered Broughton's name, when he agreed with me—or rather, I should say, pretended to do so. 'Come, Joe,' he said, 'let you and I go and speak to the girl, and if we find her willing to be gracious to the earl, we can let her go and baulk him.' Well, my dear, I came with Peter here like an ass as I was, for I ought to have mistrusted that devil, and opening the cell next to here, he said, 'Here she is. Walk in, Joe, my boy,' and in I walked, when Bayley slammed the door shut, and locked, and barred it up in a moment."

"What treachery!"

"Rather. He then looked in at me through a small crevice at the top of the door, and in his provoking way, he said—'My dear fellow, you know too much, Joe so you will have the goodness to remain here till you forget.' So saying, he left me, fully intending, no doubt, to leave me to starve in this place; for, if report among the family speaks truly, he has served several others in the same way. But owing to the way in which he had to manage the affair, you see, he had not been able to deprive me of various things I had about me, and by good luck I had the means of getting a light—some skeleton keys—a good knife, and other little matters, all of which have been the means of saving me, I think; and so, you see, Miss Jane, here I am, and I hope yet to be one too many, with your help, for old Peter."

"But," said Jane, "how have you better-ed your condition by coming into this cell?"

"Just this way. The one adjoining has

an iron bar up across the door on the outside, and that was too much for me in a little space of time to get rid of. This door is only locked, as I well know, for I heard Bayley fasten it. Of course, he knew a lock would keep you all secure, but he had his doubts of me."

"Ah, I understand now."

"In course you do. And now hold the light still, and we shall soon be able, I rather think, to give a good account of Peter Bayley's lock. Now, here you are."

Click! went the lock, and in another moment the door swung open. Nibbling Joe stepped out of the cell. Jane followed him, and ran her eyes along the passage. Suddenly she seized the arm of Nibbling Joe, and in a convulsive whisper, said—

"A light. It is coming. A light—look!"

Joe in a moment dashed his hand on the light that Jane carried, and put it out, and then they could see a broad, though sickly reflection of a light on the ceiling of the narrow passage, and it was quite clear that some one was very slowly advancing from the end of it next the staircase.

"The devil!" said Nibbling Joe.— "Come back into the cell, it's the safest place—the door is open, and we can easily watch who is coming."

They crept slowly backwards, but as they did so, the mysterious light came on.

"Stop," whispered Joe, as he found they had got back to the door of the cell, against which he struck his hand. "Hush! Not a word."

The figure bearing the light turned the corner of the passage, and then Jane saw that it was her old enemy, Mrs. Popham, with a light in one hand, and a long glittering knife in the other. The slow progress that she made arose evidently from the fact that she was only just able to walk from intoxication.

Poor Jane clung to the arms of Nibbling Joe, for she felt that at that awful hour it was something to have even such a man as that to stand by her in a moment of danger.

"Oh, God," she whispered, "she comes, as she came before, to take my life. You will protect me? Oh, say you will!"

"Why, it's Popham!"

"Oh, save me! save me!"

"Hush! Don't you put yourself out of the way. Don't you see what a sweet condition she is in. Lor bless you, a little touch will send her over, and I'll warrant

that if she once loses her feet, the old girl won't get up again in a hurry."

Mrs. Popham had just sense enough left to pause at the door of the cell that she knew Jane had been imprisoned in, but she was too far gone in intoxication to feel any surprise at finding that it was half open when it should have been locked.

"Ah," she said, "I'll have her now. I'll cut her throat, that's the way to settle her, and then one is sure—quite sure that it's all right. It's a lucky thing that I have a master-key as well as Peter. He—he don't know that. Ha! I'll cut her throat!"

Mrs. Popham laid hold of the door, but in doing so, she dropped the knife, so she let go of the door again to pick that up, and in the effort to do so she fell on her nose, and nearly smashed the lantern she had with her.

"Miss Jane," said Nibbling Joe, "come this way, and don't be afraid—let us get into the next cell; I rather think it will bother old mother Popham to get after us there."

"Oh, yes; a thousand thanks. Let us go at once."

They crept through the hole in the wall into Nibbling Joe's old lodging place; and then, by kneeling on the floor, they could see the proceedings of Mrs. Popham.

After much tumbling about, that lady had managed to get upon her feet again, and without extinguishing her light either, and pushing the door of the cell wide open she staggered into it, and balancing herself as well as she could upon her unsteady feet, she held up the light and glared around her.

"Now, my little beauty," she said, "we will soon see if a knife won't alter your looks a little. So, nothing would serve you but you must try to wheedle my Peter into making love to your baby-face—Eh?"

"Oh, that's good," whispered Nibbling Joe. "Hark! she will find out that you are gone soon."

"Come—come," added Mrs. Popham, as by staggering about with the light, and making her own shadow dance along the walls of the cell, she, in the state of intoxication she was in, fancied she was pursuing Jane. "It's no use of getting out of the way. I will have you, and no mistake. You brought yourself here just to try your smiles and your simpers, and your giggling, with Peter, and get me turned off; but I'll let you know who I am, and off comes your head as soon as I get hold of you. Take that!" Mrs. Popham made a thrust at her own shadow, and with such force that she lost her balance and fell headlong, her head striking heavily against the wall in her fall. The miserable hag was stunned. On discovering this fact, Nibbling Joe crept into the cell, and turning the body around, he coolly plunged his hand into the old woman's side pocket, with the observation:

"You are a nice beauty, you are! I'll just relieve you of the master-key you spoke of! Ah, here it is!"

"Have you got it?" asked Jane, with breathless interest.

"Yes," replied Nibbling Joe. "And now let's be off. Creep through the hole."

As Jane was about to comply, there was a sound of voices in the passage. Nibbling Joe cautiously looked out and beheld, to his surprise, Peter Bayley approaching accompanied by the Earl of Broughton.

"Back! back!" whispered Joe, "Bayley and the earl are coming!"

He dragged the inanimate body of Mrs. Popham towards the opening in the wall, and then he got backwards in to the inner cell, then clutching Mrs. Popham by the back of the neck, he held her up in a sitting posture so that she quite hid the circular orifice he had made in the wall.

"Hark!" cried Joe. "They are here!"

A flash of faint, weak light now came into the cell.

At the sight of this faint and uncertain light, Jane was silent. She felt that some dreadful crisis in her destiny had arrived, and she dreaded to picture to herself what it might end in.

The silence that ensued had something very awful in it, but it was a silence that did not last long, for Bayley broke it by raising a shout of dismay as he cried—

"Why, the cell is open!"

"Open!" said another voice which the two parties in the adjoining cell recognized as that of the Earl of Broughton. "Then she has escaped us at last."

"No—no, impossible."

"The light—give me the light, my lord," cried Bayley, "and let me look into the cell."

The light was but a poor, weak one at the best, and in the damp bad air of those cells and passages beneath the surface of the earth, it burnt so dimly that it only gave a faint, uncertain kind of glimmer. Bayley stepped within the cell and held the light above his head. The feeble rays fell upon the form of Mrs. Popham, as she was held up against the wall by the firm grasp that Joe had of the back of her neck.

"She is there!" shouted Bayley, without troubling himself to cast a second glance upon the figure. "Ha! ha! she is there."

"But how came the cell-door open?"

"I know not. It don't matter, though my lord. It is possible that I left it so from carelessness, although I don't usually do such things; but even if I did, she could not have left this place, although she might have roamed about these passages. The probability is that she has done so, and has returned at last, hopelessly, to the cell again."

"It may be so," said the earl faintly.

"Are you sure she is there?"

"Yes, I saw her. I will speak to her.—Jane, Jane, I say!"

"Answer him," whispered Joe; "place your mouth close to this little opening in the wall and answer him. There is a crevice left by the side of mother Popham's head. If they hear your voice they will be satisfied."

Jane mechanically obeyed the directions of Joe, but before she could speak, Bayley called out again, as he advanced a couple of steps into the cell—

"Speak girl, if you are there?"

"Yes, Mr. Bayley, I am here," said Jane.

"She speaks. Are you satisfied my lord?"

"I am—I am; and now—"

"No—not yet. I have a question to ask of her. I fancied that it should be yet asked again, and it may yet save her life. Jane, listen to me. Do you hear me, girl?"

"I do," said Jane.

"Then you recollect that I promised to come to you again for an answer to my proposal?"

"I do."

"I promised to save you from death, and even to give you your liberty, as well as life, if you would disclose where the cedar-box was."

"You did."

"Well, I will keep my word with you, girl. Tell me, now, where it is, and in one hour more you shall be free. Fearless Fred is food for worms, now, and if, upon his account, you persist in your obstinate silence respecting the place of concealment of the cedar-box, you are mad."

"Oh, no—no."

"What is it she says no to?" said the earl.

"Do you doubt the fact of the death of Fred, still?" said Peter Bayley.

Jane was silent.

"Say yes," whispered Joe.

"Yes—I do doubt it," said Jane. "I cannot and will not believe it."

"But," said the earl, suddenly, "life to a

young girl like you, surely, cannot be a possession destitute of all charms. You surely wish to live, do you not?" It cannot be that for the sake of keeping back a piece of information which cannot affect you to give, you will meet death itself?"

"Ah, you are my old enemy," said Jane. "I know you now. You are the Earl of Broughton."

"Fool!" said Bayley. "You have sentenced yourself, now to death."

"Not so," said the earl. "Let her still tell me where the cedar-box is, and I will consent to her being released. Nay, more, I will give her a sum of money with which she can leave England, and live in peace and comfort. What say you, Jane?"

"No—no," said Jane.

"Then you not only doom yourself to death, but another whom I have the power to murder or to save. That other, foolish girl, is Fearless Fred."

"Then he lives!"

"He does."

"Please yourself, my lord," said Bayley, bitterly. "If you think you can manage this affair in your own way better than I can do so, I will leave you here alone, if you like, with her. Don't let me be any hinderance to you. You come here, and you at once contradict what I say of you, and of others, and so you upset all my plans."

"Be patient, Bayley. When one combination fails we must just try another, that is all."

"As you please."

"But listen to reason, Bayley. You are well paid, and you have no cause to complain of me concerning other combinations and plots as they proceed. Let me try her upon this point, and it may yet succeed.

"Well—well, my lord, you may do as you please, of course. I am your humble servant."

"Jane," said the earl, "listen to me. You never believed that Fearless Fred, in whose fate you are so deeply interested, was dead.— Well, you were right—he is not dead; but he now lies under sentence of death in New-gate, and I alone can save him. My rank gives me ready access to the ear of royalty, and a word from me would save his life. I will speak that word if you will tell me where the cedar-box is to be found, with its contents."

"No," said Jane.

"Rash girl, you know not what you say. Nay, you disbelieve even this last statement, I suppose; but if you do so, and carry that disbelief too far, it will have the effect of

destroying the very person, of all others, whom you wish to save and to serve."

"I cannot trust the word of one so false as you are," said Jane.

"Then you die! Unhappy girl, you commit suicide by this foolish and criminal obstinacy as much as if you raised your hand against your own life; and you commit murder, too."

"That's a bouncer!" said Joe.

"Yes, murder, you commit; for you destroy Fearless Fred—you are his hangman as much as if you, yourself, put the rope about his neck."

"That's not so badly put," said Bayley.

"And," added the earl, "it ought to be quite clear to such a capacity as yours, that such is the fact. What are the contents of a little box to two such lives? What do you expect from those contents?"

"What do you?" said Jane.

"That is my affair. I am not in such an extremity as you are, girl, or I would not play with my life as you do. My age is three times yours; but yet I would not cast my life from me with such a reckless hand; and if there were, in all the world, one whom I loved, which I grant there is not, I would not murder that one as you would murder Fearless Fred."

"Good again," said Bayley.

"I pause for your answer, girl," added the earl.

"You have had it."

"Can it be possible that you still persevere?"

"Yes, Lord Broughton, I persevere because I feel that the man who would come with such threats as you have come with, would not scruple when he got the information he wanted to break his word."

"I will swear to you—"

"Oh, no—no, my lord! Let Heaven alone. Do not add, I pray you, to your monstrous load of guilt the horrible impiety of calling Heaven to witness your acts. Swear not, my lord."

"She is mad," said the earl.

"Now, my private opinion, my lord, is," said Peter, "that if you were to speak for a month, you would not move her resolution. She is rather obstinate."

"Then I will let her know that I am obstinate."

"Oh, no doubt it is in the family—'"

"Hush! What would you say, Bayley! Do not breath that secret for a moment. And now you—you may earn your fee."

"My fee?"

"Yes. Do the deed. I will—will wait

here, Peter Bayley, until you do the deed, for live she must not—I tell you, live she must not."

"No, my lord. I will not do the deed."

"You will not?"

"Those were my words. You start, and, no doubt, you are amazed to find that it is possible, that I, Peter Bayley, can stop short at any villany; but—but—"

"But what?"

"I cannot kill that girl."

"You cannot kill her? What can I do?"

"Kill her yourself, my lord, if you like. I tell you I cannot do it. Come a little further off and I will tell you how to manage. You have fire-arms with you, have you not?"

"Why,—a—a—"

"Yes, of course, you would not come here unarmed to see your dear friend, Peter Bayley. Well—well, let that pass—it don't matter a jot. I don't want you to trust me. But I say I will leave you here, and you can do the deed yourself, for I will not do it. You know the way out, and you will find me in my room. Your best plan is to shoot her as she kneels, for I think she is kneeling at the farther end of the cell."

"But, Bayley, I—"

"It is of no use, my lord. I will not do it; and if you don't like it, leave it alone, and come away at once."

"But I have already handed you a thousand pounds."

"Yes; and little enough, too."

"This is not the sort of dealing I expected from you, Peter Bayley. You have broken faith with me. But the death of that girl, now that she knows me, is too important a thing for me to shrink from; and if you won't do it, why—I—I—must."

"There is no must in the case, my lord."

"There is. All I ask of you now is to keep the secret, and take care that no vestige of the crime remains. I will do it—I will shoot her! I could not bear to look closely at her. I will fire at her from the door."

"Take your own course, my lord; it is not for me to aid you now, or to baulk you."

Bayley stepped aside, and the earl approached the door of the cell. He put his right foot and his right hand—that hand that carried the pistol—within the cell, and then he held up the weapon, and pointed towards the figure that he dimly saw, and fired.

The report of the pistol was quite stunning in that place, small as it was, and it so startled Jane, that she uttered a piercing shriek. As for Mrs. Popham, she fell forward on her face, and never spoke again—

The bullet had entered her brain, and killed her at once upon the spot.

"It is done!," cried the earl. "Oh, God, it is done!"

"It is," said Bayley.

"You heard her shriek?"

"Yes. There could be no mistake about that. I hope, my lord, you are now satisfied. You have done the deed, and Jane is no more. That death shriek of her's will I fear, ring in my ears for some time."

"And in mine—in mine!"

"There is no doubt about that, my lord," said Bayley, coolly. "But it is done now, and cannot be undone. Think no more of it. There is no occasion, now, to make the door of the cell fast. There is no living soul to pass out of it. I don't know how it is, but I have never felt quite the same man that I was since I saw Lolanti in the lane standing by the old gate, and beckoning to me, when I knew that half his head was off. I feel half inclined, at times, to go into the country, and live like a private gentleman."

Bayley uttered this reflection in too low a tone for the earl to hear, for he was hurrying along the narrow passage leading from the cells at the same time; and, to tell the truth, the Earl of Broughton was too much occupied by his own reflections to listen now to what Bayley was saying, if the words were not pointedly and specially addressed to him.

The hell of remorse had already commenced in the heart of the murderer!

Bayley led the way to the private room in which he always held his guilty and confidential conferences; and when there, he went direct to a cupboard, and indulged himself with a bumper of brandy.

"Is that wine?" said the earl.

"Something better, my lord. Wine won't do for us, now. We require a more potent spirit to drive out the demons of thought that at times will take possession of us. It is brandy."

"Give me some."

Bayley handed him a cup nearly full, and to his surprise, the earl drank the whole of it; and then, sinking into a chair, he said—

"I am better, now. That has revived me somewhat. It was a dreadful scene, Bayley."

"Well, I don't want to hear anything more about that; and now, my lord, we have our accounts to settle."

"Accounts? What mean you? I paid you the thousand pounds."

"You did, my lord. You paid the money like a trump; but do you know what you paid it for?"

"Yes, surely—for—for this affair."

"You paid it for leave to murder Jane, and you have murdered her accordingly.—What I want to know now is, how much are you going to give for my keeping the secret?"

"The secret?"

"Yes, the secret. You wouldn't like me to talk of it, I suppose?"

"Oh, God, no!"

"Very good, then. What are you going to give me for keeping the secret?"

"Bayley, you are a villain!"

"I know it. There are a couple of us in the room at this present time, my lord; and if the devil were to toss for us, he wouldn't much care which he won, I rather think."

"I do not like these ribald jests, Bayley."

"Very good, my lord; and so to business once again. What do you mean to give me for keeping the secret?"

"Peter Bayley, I see very well that you have got the advantage of me in this matter; and that you will use it to extort money from me. I do not see how I can help myself. I think I have paid you liberally enough; but as you will have more, I beg that you will be considerate in your demands, for I have no great command, just now, of money."

"Very good," said Bayley. "I tell you what I will do. When I want a few hundreds I will come to you."

"Hundreds?"

"Yes; I would not, with a nobleman, demean myself by asking for smaller sums.—Your lordship will be sure to hear of me."

The earl rose.

"Of that," he said, sadly, "I now make no doubt. A connexion with such a man as you are is only to be severed by death. I leave you now, Bayley, and only hope ——"

"What, my lord?"

"That you will come to me as seldom as possible, for the sight of you will recall the recollection of scenes and transactions enough to blast my peace for ever and ever."

"No. The sight of me will have no such effect, for I tell you, my lord, that you will never forget those scenes and attractions you allude to, so they will need no recalling. The events of this night are written upon your heart, and brain, and their record will never for a moment pass away."

Poor Jane's faculties had been so completely absorbed by the dreadful events that had taken place during her fearful sojourn in Peter Bayley's house, that when the earl fired the pistol at what he supposed was her, but what in reality was the insensible form of Mrs. Popham, she had uttered the shriek we have noticed, and then nearly fainted.

Joe thought that she had naturally fallen into a swoon.

"Poor thing," he thought, "it is not a bad job if she does remain in this kind of faint till these rascals are gone."

At the moment of the discharge of the pistol, Joe had let go his hold of Mrs. Popham, so that she had fallen forwards, but he did not know how the bullet had taken effect just then. All he felt certain of was that Jane had been saved, and that he himself was unhurt.

The conversation that took place subsequent to the act of murder between Bayley and the earl, was listened to by Joe with the greatest interest, for he felt how critical and dangerous his and Jane's position would be if they should come into the cell for the purpose of seeing the effect of the shot that had been fired.

If they had done so, Joe had resolved to sell his life as dearly as possible, and to do his utmost to defend Jane; for he felt that the contest that would have ensued would have been one of life or death.

What an exquisite relief to Joe was it when he heard, at length, their retiring footsteps along the passage. He listened until all trace of them had departed, and then he turned his attention to poor Jane.

"Poor thing," said Joe, "it seems a pity to try and rouse her up; but it won't do to leave her here. I said I would try and get her out of this infernal place, and I will."

"I do not sleep," said Jane, faintly.

"Sleep? no. I didn't think you did, my dear; but I did think that, girl-like, you had fainted away."

"Oh, no—no. I did not quite faint."

"But you did nearly. Well—well, it's all the better. I suppose you know what has happened?"

Jane's recollection came back to her, and she said, shudderingly—

"Ah, yes; now I recollect all, and I can perceive how this mistake has happened. It is very dreadful; but it seems like a just retribution upon that dreadful woman. She came to murder me."

"No doubt of that, Miss Jane, and she would have cut your throat as soon as look at you, if she had been sober enough to do it, and if I had not been here to stop her at that sort of fun, as in course I should; but, as it was, she was too far gone for anybody to care to interfere with her at all in the matter, you see, and so she has got settled comfortably instead of you; and here we are, and the door open."

"Oh, let us leave this dreadful place at once."

"Come on, then. But no—one moment. I will just put the old lady out of your way. Don't be impatient for a moment or two."

Joe was apprehensive that Mrs. Popham might present some fearful spectacle that might have the effect of thoroughly unmanning poor Jane, so he stepped through the opening in the wall first, before he would allow her to come, and then he saw, by the aid of a phosphorus match that he lit, the nature of the injury that had been done to Mrs. Popham.

"Dead as a herring!" he said: "and if he meant it, it was about as effectual a shot as could very well be; but I suppose chance had more to do with it than design, as he couldn't possibly have seen to take such a good aim at her in the dark."

With this, Mr. Joe pushed the dead body into the most remote corner of the cell, and then he called to Jane to come through the opening in the wall, which she immediately did.

"Now, Miss," he said, "don't you go for to fancy that you and me have nothing to do but to walk out of this place, for such isn't the fact. We may have a kind of tussle for it; but, mind you, whatever comes of me, don't you wait if you see a chance of getting off. I will do the best I can for myself, as well as for you; but if the worst, you know, should come to the worst, it is better that one of us should get away than neither, and I should like that one to be you."

"You are very good and kind to me."

"Follow me," whispered Joe. "All will depend upon who is on duty in the hall. If it's some two or three of Bayley's men that I could see, I don't think they would stand much in our way. But keep up your heart now. Mind, there is no danger yet, and, perhaps, there will be none at all."

It was known to Jane, as well as to Joe, that there was a door at the head of the staircase of great strength and thickness; but then it is admitted that he, Joe, has a key that will open it.

Beyond that door lay a passage, in which there was, night and day, one of Peter Bayley's myrmidons on duty, so that he would have to be either conquered or propitiated; and then there was another door before the passage close to the ante-door of the house could be reached.

Admitting, though, that they got that far,

they would not be very likely at that hour to encounter any one.

It was the sentinel that was the most difficult part of the business to get over, and was towards discovering who he was of Bayley's men that Joe now felt his endeavour should be directed.

When Jane had been conducted into the dungeon-like abode by Bayley, the stone steps that she was now ascending had appeared to her to be very few in quantity. How different was the feeling that possessed her now as she slowly crept up them after Joe. She thought them interminable, and that she should never get upon the level at the top of them, and leave that dreary dungeon abode behind her.

"Have you reached the door?" she said.

"Not yet."

"Alas!—alas!"

"Nay, now, don't give up when we are so far in safety. Here is the door at last. Confound it!"

"What has happened?"

"I have dropped the key, that's all. Don't be alarmed, though. I will soon find it.—Did you not hear it fall?"

"I did. Something touched my foot. It is here—I have it."

In the intense darkness, Jane had some difficulty in finding Joe's hand into which to place the key; but she did so at last, and he uttered an expression of satisfaction at getting it.

It would be quite impossible to give any idea by words of the state of great anxiety that beset Jane during this time. Each minute appeared to be an hour of delay, and she was perpetually upon the point of urging Joe to be more rapid in his movements, at the same time that she felt she ought not to do so, and that all he was doing was for the best, and that she might trust his judgment in the matter most implicitly and completely.

"The lock is rusty," said Joe.

"You cannot open it—Oh, you cannot open it!"

"Hush! not so loud. The door, they say, is thick enough to stop all sounds; but still it is possible some one may be close enough to it to fancy they hear, amid such a stillness as seems to be in the house, a voice, and if so, we are lost."

At these words, Jane was silent. She shook violently, though, and her sense of hearing seemed to have become preternaturally acute, for she heard the key in the lock so plainly, that it was quite painful to listen to the slight grating sound it made.

"You cannot unlock it," said Jane, in such a faint whisper, that it was quite out of question it could reach any other ears than his.

"Yes—yes."

The lock went back with a sudden sound, and Joe paused immediately to listen if he had given any alarm.

All was still.

"Jane," he said, "Jane?"

"Yes—oh, yes. I am here."

"I begin to think that the usual sentinel is not behind this door."

"You think so? Oh, what a hope!"

"Yes, I do think so; and if it be so, it arises from the fact that Peter has sent all witnesses of the earl's presence in the house out of the way, so that he might have all that secret to himself."

"It must be so."

"It looks like it, I confess; but do you go down a step or two, while I open the door carefully."

"Yes, I will—I will. Much as I dread even the return of a step or two to this dreadful place below, I will go."

"It will only be for a moment. Take courage. Every instant now convinces me more and more that there is no one here."

At this moment, when they thought that escape was almost in their grasp, and when Joe had the key actually in the lock of the door, that they suddenly heard a footstep in the passage beyond.

Joe paused.

"Oh, we are lost!" said Jane.

"Hush!" he whispered. "Not a word. It may be of no consequence, after all. Do not speak, I beg of you."

Jane was silent, but from excitement, her heart beat so violently as to be exceedingly painful, and she pressed both her hands upon it for the purpose of trying to still its tumultuous throbbings.

Joe placed his ear close to the panel of the door, and listened intently to every sound.

The footstep was a rough one, and suddenly it ceased, and the voice of Bayley was heard, saying—

"Hilloa! Is this the way you keep watch? Asleep, idiot!"

Both Jane and Joe knew that voice.— There was no such thing as mistaking it after having once heard it. It was the voice of Peter Bayley! Yes, there they were, all but in the power of their most dreaded enemy.

For a moment poor Jane thought that she would have fallen there and then fainted upon the stone steps leading from the cells, but by one great effort she preserved herself from that fate, for she felt that if anything was to be done for her preservation it would only be by taking care to preserve all her faculties about her.

Joe was staggered by this unexpected appearance of Peter Bayley, and for the moment he hardly knew what to do; but he stood with the master-key in his hand, that he had taken from Mrs. Popham, as if that would be a sufficient weapon with which to fight the matter out with Peter Bayley.

It was a moment of suspense.

What reply the man, who had been upon duty at that spot and fallen asleep upon his post, made to Peter Bayley, neither Joe nor Jane heard, for he spoke in a very low voice; but in another moment the harsh grating tones of Bayley's voice came again to their ears quite plainly.

"Not asleep, wretch?" he said.

Then they heard the man speak.

"No, Mr. Bayley. I was deep in thought, I admit, but I was not asleep."

"You were, vagabond!"

"Excuse me, Mr. Bayley, for contradicting you, but I was not. The fact is, nobody is at all likely to sleep in your service although one might do so better than in any other's."

"What do you mean by that?"

"Why, sir, I just mean that you are always so wide awake, that I don't think much harm could possibly happen if every one else in the house was to go to sleep."

"Oh, indeed!"

It was evident enough, by the alteration in Bayley's tone, that he was a little modified by the politic compliment of the man who was on duty.

"Hark you," he added; "don't let me catch you at this sort of thing again, or it will fare worse with you."

"No, sir."

"Now, tell me, have you—have you."— Bayley did not know very well how to shape his question, and he paused for a moment before he added, "Have you heard any sound from the cells since I was there?"

"Not the least, Mr. Bayley."

"But have you listened?"

"Oh, dear, yes, Mr. Bayley. I keep my ears open always."

"But not your eyes. Ha! you manage to listen while you are asleep, do you, curse you?"

As he spoke, all the natural ferocity of Bayley's character seemed to return to him, and Jane and Joe heard the rattle of his key in the lock in the door. Poor Jane gave her self up for lost. but not so Joe. He had quite recovered from the first state of panic into which he had been thrown, and now coolly and calmly did all he could.

It was strange how none of Bayley's people thought that, single-handed, it would be at all possible to get the better of the rascal. By some means he had succeeded in impressing upon them, one and all, the idea that anything in the shape of a personal struggle with him would be one of the most hopeless things in all the world.

It was quite a pity that, without giving the matter much thought, Joe joined in the idea.

If such had not been the impression upon the mind of Joe, there was nothing in the world to hinder him from trying his strength upon Peter Bayley.

There would have been some evident advantages, too, upon the side of Joe, for he could have taken the rascal at unawares, and certainly dealt him the first blow, which, in a contest of that nature, would have been one half the battle.

Joe had a knife, too ; and he had suffered quite enough from Bayley, and knew the villain quite well enough, to enable him to shake off any scruples he might otherwise have had about raising it ; but the idea of fighting the affair out with Peter Bayley, unless he could not help such a course, did not come pleasantly home to Joe's comprehension at all.

As for Jane, of course she felt that she could not doubt the greater tact and experience of the man who was with her under such circumstances.

The brief conversation that Bayley had had with his drowsy sentinel had just given Joe time to lock the door again, which it will be remembered he had succeeded in unlocking with the master-key he had obtained from the delightful Mrs. Popham. It was a great object gained not to excite Bayley's suspicion that there was anything amiss at present.

Joe then whispered to Jane as he laid his hand upon her arm gently—

" Back—back—back—"

" Oh, no—no."

" Yes. I say. You must. I will tell you what to do. We must get down the steps again. Hush—hush ! He comes—he comes !"

There was the flash of a light, and Jane, feeling that if she did place her fortune and life in the hands of Joe, the only thing she could do was to obey his instructions, retreated with a heavy heart down those steps a-

gain, which she thought she had left for ever a few moments since.

" Death," she said, in a low tone. " Death is even preferable to falling into the hands of Peter Bayley."

" I know it," said Joe.

The flash of light that had come through the murky atmosphere of that place came from a little oil-lamp that Peter Bayley carried to light him on his way.

It gave but a small light at any time, that lamp, even in the purest atmosphere, but the moment the little flame encountered the damps of the cells and the close and dank regions around them, it gradually dwindled down.

Bayley thought it was going out ; and uttering a malediction upon it, he paused for a moment to look at it.

That pause enabled Joe and Jane to reach the foot of the stone staircase, and to run towards the open door of Jane's cell, so that they were fairly enough out of Bayley's way for the moment, at all events.

" Curses on the light !" muttered Bayley, as he watched the little flame ; but then, as he saw that after reaching rather a low point of combustion, it got no worse, he at once attributed it to its right cause.

" It is the bad air here, he muttered. " Well—well, so long as it don't go out, it will do, and the air is good enough for them that I choose to place here to breathe it."

" What shall we do ?" whispered Jane.

" I don't know, yet."

" But our discovery is certain."

" Well, it does seem like it. rather."

" You are a man. You will not, surely, let yourself be conquered by another man ? You will raise your arm against that monster in human shape, even for my sake, as well as your own ?"

" I will."

" And I, too, will defend myself. Oh, that I had some weapon with which to do so effectually !"

These words of Jane recalled Joe to the obvious fact that he might, if he chose, surely, even with some chance of success, fight with Peter Bayley, and be sought for the handle of the knife that he had so opportunely taken from Mrs. Popham.

" Yes," he said, " I will fight."

" Hush ! Oh, hush ! He approaches !" whispered Jane.

They both crouched down close to the door of the cell, in which lay the dead body of Mrs. Popham, and they heard Bayley muttering to himself, as he came slowly on.

" Curses on him ! I wish he had not done it ; but I must dig a hole in the floor of the cell, and bury her, and every time I come down here, I shall feel—what I feel now !"

The wretch shook perceptibly, and had to lean against the damp stone wall for support.

" Why didn't I stay his hand ?" he said. " I might have done it. If I had said no to the deed, of course, there would have been an end of it, and he dared not have raised a finger against her ; but I let him do it—yes, I let him do it, and now I feel half mad at the thought 'hat I did do so. God, I—I—shall never forget it !"

This was, probably, the first time in his life, that Peter Bayley had had any feeling of remorse for a deed of blood ; but, somehow, the beauty, the youth, the innocence, and the rare and marvellous courage of Jane, had awakened, even in the heart of that wicked man, a feeling of respect and admiration ; and now that she was gone, he fully believed, in consequence of the pistol-shot of the Earl of Broughton he felt that he would give anything to restore her to existence again.

And yet, what would Bayley have done, had he been assured that Jane lived ?

If the young creature had stepped forward, and said, " I am here ! The bullet intended for me entered another bosom !" what would Bayley then have done ?

The possibility is, that the feelings towards her of pity and of admiration, brought into existence by the presumed fact of her death, would have vanished, and he would have thought only of how he was to turn her continued existence to account against the Earl of Broughton, for the purpose of extorting money from him.

Again Bayley wiped the streaming drops of cold perspiration from his face, and then he said—

" Who would have thought it that Lolanti, whom I once knew so well should fall by my hand at last, and that the young girl whom he so often pointed out to me should be a bleeding corpse in one of my cells ?"

Neither Jane nor Joe ventured to say a word, now, although they plainly heard all that Peter Bayley uttered, and were deeply interested in it.

" Well—well," said Bayley, at last, making an effort to recover his usual state of indifference to the fate of others. " It is done, now, and it cannot be undone ; but never shall I set my foot within this place without a shudder as I think of Jane ; and there will be times when, amid the dim shad-

ows that are here, I shall shudder to think that her fair and delicate spirit may be haunting me, and gazing at me with those eyes that even now seem as if they beamed on me."

As he drew this imaginative picture to himself, the agitation of Bayley increased and he staggered back a pace or two, crying—

" No—no, Jane ! I tell you I did not do it. It was the earl—It was your uncle who did the deed ! Help ! help ! mercy ! No ! no ! Hush ! Oh, what is all this ? Am I mad ?"

" Your uncle, did he say ?" whispered Joe, in so gentle a voice, close to the ear of Jane, that she started at the first sound.

" He did," she replied.

" But it was the Earl of Broughton, Peter said."

" Hush ! hush ! He speaks again."

" Yes," said Joe, " and he has already spoken enough to give me an idea that, I think, is a good one."

Bayley spoke again, in a weak voice.

" That is past," he said. " What was it that, for the moment, seemed to drive me to the verge of distraction ? Was it the consciousness that I had to do this dreadful night's work yet—to bury the body ? Yes, that is the worst of it. It was easy to fire the shot that did the deed, but it is not easy to hide the evidence of it, I ought to have made him come and bury the body."

" Bayley took the lamp from the little iron bracket.

" Jane ?" whispered Joe.

" Yes, I hear."

" When I say to you ' Now !' I wish you to advance, and to say in a deep and solemn voice, ' Peter Bayley !"

" Ah ! I comprehend."

" I thought you would. Our only chance, now, is to terrify Bayley with the idea that it is your spirit he sees before him. In his present frame of mind, that will not be at all difficult. It is far better than killing him, I think, and I suppose you will think the same."

" Oh, yes—yes !"

" You will do it, then ?"

" I will—I will !"

" Hush ! Not so loud."

Peter Bayley advanced now slowly, and with such a staggering step, that, if they had not been well aware from his previous conduct that such was not the fact, both Joe and Jane would have thought him under the influence of liquor ; but such was not the case. It was the mind of the villain that had experienced such a shock as it had not known before.

The distance he had to traverse, before reaching the spot upon which were Joe and Jane, was about twenty-five paces; but Bayley crept rather than walked on, so that he was much longer in arriving near them than under ordinary circumstances he would have been.

The door of the cell, too, was wide open —that is to say, it was at right angles with the opening—so that both Jane and Joe were hidden most effectually by it from the sight of Bayley, although he held the lamp about a foot above his head, and with a gaze of intense fear looked right before him, as though he fully expected to catch a glance of some horrible object.

" Now!" said Joe, in a low tone.

Jane had nerved herself for the part she had to play, and the circumstance that most had enabled her to do so, was the one that, if she did not do it effectually, the death of Bayley would be the only alternative. Her gentle, womanly nature revolted at the idea of even the death of such a man as Peter Bayley.

The moment Joe gave her the signal, she stepped from behind the door, and appeared right in the path of Bayley. She held up both her arms, and in solemn tones, she said—

" Peter Bayley! Peter Bayley!"

The already excited imagination of Bayley was well prepared for all the effect that this seeming apparition of the murdered Jane had upon it, and with a horrible yell he fell backwards to the stone floor, dashing the lamp to pieces in his fall.

All was still.

" That has done it," said Joe. " He is dead."

" Dead?"

" Yes. I heard his head go with such a crush against the stones, that if it stands that it will stand anything. How dark it is ! Where are you, Jane?—where are you?"

" Here I am—here," said Jane, in a faint voice.

Nibbling Joe took her by the hand. and led her carefully along the narrow passage, and up the staircase to the door leading to the hall. On reaching the latter, Joe peeped carefully through a small hole, and perceived that the guard had fallen asleep on his post. On making this joyful discovery, Joe beckoned his companion to follow him carefully, and they were soon out of the dreadful habitation of the thief-taker.

CHAPTER XIII.

At the time that Fearless Fred entered the house of the Chancellor, the latter was engaged in listening to the representations of Mrs. Block, who had come to London on purpose to plead the cause of the celebrated highwayman.

The Lord Chancellor had previously been acquainted with the lady, on account of some good service that her husband had done for him in other days. Hence he gave her an audience more cheerfully. As the lady proceeded with her narration, the Chancellor evinced an interest which the simple facts in her story were, in the opinion of Mrs. Block, hardly sufficient to account for.

It so happened that during his stay with Mrs. Block, Fearless Fred had given that lady a full history of his early life. He had told her that he was a foundling, and had mentioned the date of the period at which he was discovered in a common tavern, as stated at the opening of our narrative. This part of her story aroused the attention of the Lord Chancellor, in so marked a manner that Mrs. Block was surprised at the emotion he betrayed. When she had concluded, he put several questions, which she apparently answered to his satisfaction, as he cried out—" It is surely my own son! This person must be saved at all events. A child answering precisely the description of Fearless Fred was stolen from us at the period you mention, and there cannot be the shadow of a doubt that this highwayman is my son."

Mrs. Block expressed her gratification at this discovery, and regretted that the young man was not at hand in order that the Chancellor might have an opportunity to identify him. It was while they were in the midst of this conversation that a considerable bustle was heard at the door, attended with angry exclamations. The Chancellor inquired what was the matter, and was informed that a young stranger insisted upon seeing the Lord Chancellor, and that the servants were endeavoring to prevent his entrance. Mrs. Block started up in agitation, and the Chancellor ordered that the stranger should be immediately admitted to his presence. In another moment Fearless Fred rushed into the apartment with the cedar-box in his hand. The Chancellor was informed that this was the individual about whom he had been speaking, and he immediately fell to questioning Fred about his history, especially the early part of it. Fred looked from Mrs. Block to the Chancellor.

and seemed much at a loss to understand the meaning of all he saw and heard. At length the Chancellor embraced Fred, and called him his son. The latter was, of course much surprised, and Mrs. Block congratulated him upon having found a father. Finally the cedar-box was produced and opened, which contained papers that established the claims of Jane to the estates of the Earl of Broughton, and which proved her to be a Countess in her own right.

Little needs to be added. Through the influence of the Chancellor, a full pardon was obtained for Fearless Fred, who entered at once, upon a course of honor and prosperity, while Jane, whose escape with Nibbling Joe was perfectly successful, became united in marriage with the man whom she had so long and so fervently loved. We need not say that the happiness of the parties was complete, and that this union put an end to the wandering and uncertain career of FEARLESS FRED.